SHADOWS BETWEEN THOUGHTS

THE ETHAN REEVES WEREWOLF DETECTIVE SERIES
BOOK FIVE

RAE STONEHOUSE

LIVE FOR EXCELLENCE PRODUCTIONS

PROLOGUE: ECHOES IN THE DARKNESS

The abandoned halls of Daybridge Maximum Security Psychiatric Hospital whispered with the weight of its dark history. Once a beacon of healing, the sprawling gothic structure now stood as a decaying reminder of the unspeakable acts that had taken place within its walls.

For Ryan Matthews, Jojo Lang, and Jason Reeves, the allure of uncovering the hospital's secrets had been too powerful to resist. As professional ghost hunters, they had ventured into the building's shadowy depths, armed with cameras, voice recorders, and an insatiable curiosity for the paranormal. Little did they know that their investigation would awaken a malevolent force that had lain dormant for decades.

On that fateful night, the ghost hunters had made their way through the twisting corridors, their flashlights casting eerie shadows on the peeling walls. The air grew colder with each step, and a sense of unease crept over them like a suffocating blanket.

In a dimly lit room that had once served as a doctor's office, they discovered a trove of patient files and medical journals. The musty papers held dark secrets, hinting at unethical experiments and twisted practices carried out in the name of science. As they delved deeper into the disturbing records, a sudden gust of icy wind extinguished their lights, plunging them into darkness.

Disembodied whispers filled the room, growing louder and more urgent with each passing second. The ghost hunters froze, their hearts pounding in their chests as an invisible presence seemingly surrounded them. Ryan, the leader of the group, tried to rationalize the experience, but deep down, he knew they had stumbled upon something far more sinister than a simple haunting.

Jason, driven by an inexplicable urge, reached out to touch one of the old medical devices. As his fingers brushed against the cold metal, a jolt of energy surged through his body, and visions of unspeakable horrors flooded his mind. He saw patients strapped to gurneys, their screams echoing through the halls as a shadowy figure loomed over them, wielding glinting surgical tools.

Jojo, the tech expert, frantically tried to capture the paranormal activity on her modified camera, but the device malfunctioned, its screen flickering with distorted images of twisted faces and ghostly apparitions. The very walls seemed to pulse with a malevolent energy, as if the hospital itself was alive and angry at their intrusion.

Overwhelmed by the intensity of the encounter, the ghost hunters fled, their footsteps echoing through the abandoned corridors. But as they raced toward the exit, a sinister force took hold, determined to keep them within its grasp. Doors slammed shut, trapping them in a labyrinth of darkness, and an unearthly howl reverberated through the building, shaking them to their core.

From that moment on, Ryan, Jojo, and Jason were never seen again. Or were they? Their disappearance sparked whispers of the hospital's curse and tales of the vengeful spirits that roamed its halls. The ghost hunters' families were left with unanswered questions and a growing sense of dread, desperate for any clue that might lead to their loved ones' whereabouts.

Now, two weeks after their vanishing, the case has landed on the desk of Ethan Reeves, a seasoned detective with a secret of his own. As a werewolf, Ethan possesses heightened senses and supernatural abilities that have served him well in his investigations. Alongside his trusted partner, Alice, he must venture into the depths of Daybridge Max and confront the malevolent forces that lurk within.

But as Ethan delves deeper into the mystery, he realizes that the disappearance of the ghost hunters is just the beginning. A twisted web of secrets, born from the hospital's dark past, threatens to ensnare them all. With time running out and the shadows closing in, Ethan must use all his skills and cunning to unravel the truth, save the missing ghost hunters, and confront the evil that stalks the halls of Daybridge Max.

For in the abandoned wards and hidden laboratories, something wicked has awakened, hungry for vengeance and ready to unleash its fury upon the world. And only Ethan Reeves stands between the darkness and the unsuspecting souls beyond the hospital's cursed walls.

COPYRIGHT

Published by Live For Excellence Productions

ISBN:

Ebook: 978-1-998591-40-4

Paperback: 978-1-998591-41-1

Audiobook: 978-1-998591-42-8

CHAPTER ONE

THE DECISION

THE FLUORESCENT LIGHTS OF RYAN MATTHEWS' office flickered, casting intermittent shadows across the wall of monitors. Each screen displayed a different angle of Daybridge Max, its decrepit façade a stark reminder of decades of abandonment. The security feeds, obtained through questionably legal means, showed the building in various states of decay: collapsed corridors, rooms filled with broken furniture, and graffiti-covered walls that seemed to shift in the evening light.

Ryan leaned back in his chair, running his fingers through his graying hair as he studied the building's blueprint for the hundredth time. Dark circles under his eyes betrayed countless sleepless nights spent researching the hospital's history. Red marks dotted the blueprints, each indicating a reported supernatural occurrence – too many to be coincidence.

"You're obsessing again," Jojo Lang said from the doorway, her laptop balanced precariously on one arm while she adjusted her thick-rimmed glasses with her free hand. The gentle hum of her custom-built EMF detector filled the silence between them. "But I get it. This one's different."

The way she said "different" carried weight. They both knew this wasn't just another haunted house or abandoned asylum. The readings they'd gotten from their preliminary scans had nearly fried their equipment – something Jojo had never seen in her fifteen years of paranormal investigation.

Ryan nodded without looking up. "Thirty-seven documented deaths in the experimental ward alone. Whatever happened in there, it left a mark." He tapped a particular spot on the blueprint – the notorious Ward 7. "And those are just the ones they bothered to record. God knows how many more disappeared without a trace."

"And you're sure we're ready for this?" Jojo moved into the room, setting her laptop beside the blueprints. Her screen displayed a complex array of wavelength patterns that made no logical sense. "The equipment's been acting strange just from our preliminary scans. Last night, my primary scanner picked up voices speaking in Latin – backward."

Ryan's hand unconsciously moved to the scar on his neck – a souvenir from the Portland incident that had changed everything. "That's exactly why we need to do this," he replied, finally meeting her gaze. The determination in his eyes masked an underlying fear they both felt. "Before I saw what I saw in that house in Portland, I would have dismissed all of this as electromagnetic interference or structural settling. But now..."

"Now you need answers," Jojo finished his sentence. "We all do." She glanced at her own reflection in one of the darkened monitors, remembering the spirit that had followed her home from their last investigation, the one that still whispered to her in her dreams.

The door creaked open again, and Jason Reeves stepped in, his young face alight with barely contained excitement. "The van's packed. I double-checked all the equipment like you asked, Jojo." There was something in his pocket that he kept touching nervously – a family heirloom, he'd said, though he never showed it to anyone.

Ryan studied the newest member of their team. There was something about Jason that reminded him of himself before that night in Portland – eager, skeptical, yet hoping to find something that would change everything. But there was something else too, something in the way the equipment reacted when Jason was nearby, in the way shadows seemed to bend around him when he thought no one was looking.

"Did you pack the new thermal cameras?" Ryan asked, rolling up the blueprints with deliberate care. "The ones with the upgraded infrared sensors?"

"All six of them," Jason confirmed. "And the EVP recorders with the quantum tunneling modifications Jojo designed. Everything's ready." His enthusiasm barely masked an undercurrent of anxiety that Ryan recognized all too well.

The overhead light flickered again, and for a moment, just a moment, all three of them cast shadows in different directions. None of them mentioned it, but they all noticed. In their line of work, even the smallest details could mean the difference between life and death.

"Then I guess it's time," Ryan said, standing up and gathering his papers. "Daybridge Max has kept its secrets for long enough. Tonight, we find out what really happened in Ward 7."

As they left the office, the monitors behind them continued to show the hospital's empty corridors. In one screen, barely noticeable in the grainy footage, a shadow moved against the wind, waiting.

❧

CHAPTER TWO

DARK WELCOME

THE SUN WAS SETTING behind the Daybridge Maximum Security
Psychiatric Hospital when they arrived, painting the building's broken
windows in shades of blood red. Ryan watched the colors fade from
the passenger seat, his hand instinctively touching the silver pendant
around his neck – a habit he'd developed after his first encounter with
the unexplainable. The pendant had belonged to his grandmother,
who'd warned him about places like this, places where the veil
between worlds grew thin.

Through the windshield, Daybridge Maxis Victorian architecture
loomed against the darkening sky, its weathered gargoyles keeping
their eternal watch. Decades of neglect had transformed what was
once a beacon of hope into a monument to suffering. Vines crawled up
the brick walls like grasping fingers, and several windows gaped open
like screaming mouths.

"EMF's already going crazy," Jojo announced from the back of the
van, where she was monitoring their baseline readings. Her equipment chirped and whined in protest. "Whatever's in there, it's
active." She adjusted several dials, frowning at the erratic patterns on
her screen. "These readings... they're unlike anything I've ever seen.

It's as if the entire building is generating its own electromagnetic field."

The van's headlights illuminated a rusty sign that read "Daybridge Maximum Security Psychiatric Hospital - Est. 1887." Below it, barely visible through years of weathering, someone had spray-painted "ABANDON HOPE" in faded red letters.

Ryan killed the engine, and silence fell over the team. The hospital loomed before them, five stories of gothic architecture and dark history. Thick iron bars, remnants of the building's days as a high-security psychiatric facility, crisscrossed every window like skeletal fingers. Some bars were bent outward, as if something had forced its way through them with impossible strength JoJo noticed that despite decades of exposure, the bars showed no signs of rust – only deep scratch marks that caught the fading light. Wind whistled through the cracks in the walls, creating a sound almost like distant weeping. Or perhaps, JoJo thought as she studied those unmarred iron bars, it wasn't the wind at all. The bars had been designed to keep patients in, but she wondered if their true purpose had been to keep something else out – something that had found its way in anyway.

"Remember," Ryan said, turning to face his team, his features cast in shadow by the dying light. "We stay together. No wandering off, no solo heroics. Whatever's in there has had decades to grow stronger." His hand unconsciously touched the scar on his neck. "This isn't like our other investigations. The reports I've read... people have disappeared here. Good people. Experienced investigators."

Jason shifted uncomfortably in his seat, and Ryan noticed him touching something in his pocket – a gesture that seemed more like seeking reassurance than checking equipment. The object made a slight metallic sound, like chains or links clicking together.

As they unloaded their gear, the last rays of sunlight disappeared, plunging the hospital grounds into darkness broken only by their flashlights. Dead leaves skittered across the cracked pavement, and somewhere in the distance, a crow called out a warning. The main entrance doors hung askew on their hinges, creating a maw-like opening into the building's interior. The brass handles were tarnished green with age, and Jason could have sworn he saw handprints appearing and disappearing in the oxidation.

JoJo's flashlight beam caught movement in one of the second-floor windows – a shadow, quick and deliberate, passing behind the dirty glass. It wasn't the formless darkness of a cloud passing overhead; this shadow had shape, had purpose. For a brief moment, she thought she saw it pause and turn toward them.

"Did you see that?" she whispered, her pendant growing inexplicably cold against her skin.

"Log it," Ryan replied, his voice steady despite the chill that ran down his spine. "Time, location, description. We document everything." He checked his watch: 7:42 PM. "Jojo, start the thermal imaging. Jason, get the EVP recorder running."

As they crossed the threshold into Daybridge Max, the air temperature dropped ten degrees. Their flashlight beams cut through decades of dust, revealing a stark administrative checkpoint with its bulletproof glass partition still intact. Behind the glass, abandoned logbooks lay open, their pages yellow and brittle with age. The first security gate, a massive iron barrier with bars as thick as JoJo's wrist, stood partially open, its heavy-duty electronic lock long dead. Beyond it lay the processing office where new inmates were once photographed, searched, and stripped of their belongings. The second security gate, even more formidable than the first, sealed off the main wing. Its reinforced bars were marked with deep gouges near the locking mechanism, as if something had tried to claw its way through. The institutional mint-green paint on the concrete walls had peeled away in sheets, revealing the cold gray beneath. Their footsteps echoed off the bare floors, the sound bouncing between the metal gates and empty guard stations, creating a hollow percussion that seemed to pulse in time with their heartbeats.

"It's just the wind," Jojo said, but her voice lacked conviction. Her equipment was now emitting a high-pitched whine that set everyone's teeth on edge. "But these readings... they're off the charts. Something here is generating more energy than should be possible."

Ryan checked his equipment one last time, his experienced hands moving over the familiar devices. "Remember why we're here. Whatever happens, we find the truth." He didn't add what they all knew: that sometimes the truth came at a terrible price.

As they moved deeper into the hospital's darkness, none of them noticed the shadows beginning to move against the walls, flowing against the light of their beams, watching and waiting. The shadows seemed to pulse with a life of their own, and in their depths, something ancient stirred. Daybridge Max Security Hospital had been waiting for them, and now they were here.

In Ryan's pocket, his phone silently died, its screen showing one final message that no one had sent: "Welcome home."

❧

CHAPTER THREE
THE MISSING

THE MORNING SUN did little to warm Ethan Reeves' office as he stared at the three photographs spread across his desk. Missing persons cases weren't unusual in his line of work, but something about these made his wolf stir beneath his skin.

"It's been seventy-two hours," Margaret Matthews said, her fingers trembling as she touched her son's photo. Ryan Matthews smiled back from the image, his investigator's badge gleaming. "The police say they can't enter the Daybridge Maximum Security Hospital without permits. Something about structural hazards."

Alice Chen leaned against the doorframe, her detective's instincts already cataloging the details. The second photo showed a young Asian woman with thick-rimmed glasses - Jojo Lang, tech expert. The third was...

Ethan's hand froze over the last photograph. "Jason Reeves," he said, his voice barely a whisper. The familiar features of his cousin stared back at him, and suddenly the case became personal. "He never told me he was working with a ghost hunting team."

"They were broadcasting live on their channel," Margaret continued, pulling up a video on her tablet. "This was their last transmission."

The footage was grainy, shot in night vision. Ryan's voice came through clearly: "We're entering the administrative section now. The EMF readings are off the charts..." Static interference cut through the audio. "...something's wrong with the equipment..." More static, then Jojo's voice: "These energy signatures... they're not normal..." Then Jason: "There's something in here with—"

The video cut to black.

Alice moved closer, studying the timestamp. "That was three nights ago, during the full moon." She gave Ethan a meaningful look.

"Mrs. Matthews," Ethan said, standing up. "I'll need access to all their research on the Daybridge Max Security. Every detail, no matter how small."

"Ryan kept everything in his office," she replied, handing him a key. "It's become something of an obsession since Portland."

After Margaret left, Alice closed the door. "You're not telling me everything. What happened in Portland?"

Ethan pulled out an old case file. "Two years ago, Ryan Matthews investigated a haunted house in Portland. He went in a skeptic. Came out..." Ethan showed her a photograph of Ryan in a hospital bed, a distinctive scar across his neck. "Whatever he encountered there changed him. He started gathering evidence about supernatural phenomena, focusing on places with high concentrations of unexplained events."

"Like Daybridge," Alice said.

"Daybridge Max Security isn't just any abandoned hospital," Ethan replied, pulling up the building's history on his computer. "It was a maximum-security facility for the criminally insane. But there were rumors about unauthorized experiments in the restricted wings. The kind of experiments that leave marks on reality itself."

"And your cousin?"

Ethan's jaw tightened. "Jason always wanted to be part of this world. The supernatural, the unexplained. But I kept him away to protect him. He's only nineteen, Alice. And now..."

"We'll find them," Alice assured him, but her expression was grim. "But Ethan, you should know - Daybridge has a history with your kind. In the 1950s, there were reports of werewolf patients being held there for study."

Ethan stared at the old hospital through his office window, its gothic spires jutting against the morning sky like accusing fingers. Something moved behind one of the barred windows - a shadow where no shadow should be.

"Then we better hope they're still alive," he said, his eyes flickering gold for a moment, revealing the predator within. "Because if they're not, Daybridge is going to learn why you never harm a werewolf's family." His voice deepened with barely suppressed rage. "Jason is my blood. And in our world, when you take a wolf's family member, you face the entire pack. We don't stop. We don't show mercy. And we don't rest until we've torn apart everything in our path."

Alice checked her weapon, making sure the silver bullets were loaded. "When do we start?"

"Tonight," Ethan replied, studying the lunar calendar on his wall. "The moon is still full enough. I'll need my wolf's senses in there."

As they prepared to leave, Ethan's phone buzzed. A text message from an unknown number showed a single image - security camera footage from inside the Daybridge, Max Security, timestamped ten minutes ago. In it, three figures could be seen moving through a corridor, but their shapes were wrong, distorted, as if something else was wearing their faces.

The message below read: "They're still here. But they're not alone anymore."

CHAPTER FOUR

ECHOES OF THE PAST

THE ARCHIVES of the City Records Office smelled of dust and deteriorating paper. Ethan and Alice sat surrounded by stacks of files, their laptops casting a blue glow in the dimly lit basement room. The archival documents about Daybridge Max painted a disturbing picture with each new file they opened.

"Look at this," Alice said, carefully unfolding a yellowed newspaper from 1953. "Dr. Mark Bl ackburn appointed as Head of Psychiatric Research. According to this, he specialized in "treating' supernatural beings." She passed Ethan a photograph showing a tall, austere man in a white coat, standing before Daybridge's Max Security iron gates. His smile didn't reach his eyes.

Ethan's fingers trembled slightly as he read through a classified internal memo. "They weren't just treating them. Listen to this: "Subject 23-W exhibits extraordinary regenerative capabilities under extreme duress. Recommend increasing voltage in next trial. Silver-based restraints proving effective.'" He pushed back from the table, running a hand through his hair. "They were torturing werewolves, trying to understand our healing abilities."

Alice pulled up another document on her laptop. "It gets worse. Hospital admission records from 1950 to 1965 show over three hundred patients classified as "non-human entities.' But the death certificates..." She turned the screen toward him. "Only forty-seven documented deaths. The rest just vanish from the records."

"Here's something," Ethan said, opening a crumbling leather journal. "Dr. Blackburn's personal notes. December 12, 1957: "The barrier grows thinner with each experiment. We can hear them now, whispering from the other side. The subjects' pain creates a resonance that weakens the veil between worlds. Director Hayes objects to the methods, but he doesn't understand the magnitude of our work. We aren't just studying these creatures – we're opening a door.'"

Alice leaned forward, her detective's instincts sharp. "A door to what?"

Before Ethan could answer, a photograph slipped from between the journal's pages. It showed a group of doctors standing in what appeared to be a surgical theater. Behind them, barely visible in the shadows, a dark figure loomed, its form distorted and wrong.

"There's more," Ethan continued, his voice tight. "March 3, 1958: "Lost another orderly today. They keep wandering into Ward D, despite explicit instructions to avoid the lower levels. The entity in Cell 237 grows stronger with each disappearance. Hayes threatens to shut us down, but it's too late now. They're already here.'"

Alice pulled up the hospital's blueprints on her laptop. "Ward D isn't on any official floor plan. Look – the building specs show a subbasement, but these maintenance logs reference five levels below ground."

Ethan found a staff list from 1960. "In three months, they lost twenty-eight employees. Official cause: "voluntary resignation.' But look at this internal report: "Staff members report hearing voices calling their names. Increased incidents of sleepwalking toward restricted areas. Subject in Cell 237 requires additional silver reinforcement to containment chamber.'"

"The hospital closed suddenly in 1965," Alice noted, scanning through closure documents. "No explanation given. They transferred all standard patients to other facilities, but there's no record of what happened to the supernatural inmates."

A small red notebook caught Ethan's eye. Inside, in shaky handwriting: "Final Log, June 15, 1965. They're everywhere now. The shadows move on their own. The silver barriers in Ward D have failed. Hayes is dead – found him in 237, or what was left of him. The things we brought through... God forgive us. We thought we could control them. Contain them. Study them. But we only made them stronger. I'm sealing the lower levels. The entities are too powerful now, tied to the building itself, feeding off decades of pain and fear. If anyone finds this, stay out. Some doors should never be opened. -M. Blackburn"

"That's the last record of him," Alice said quietly. "Marcus Blackburn disappeared that day, along with sixteen other staff members."

Ethan closed the notebook, his wolf senses picking up a faint scent of decay from its pages. "They didn't just study supernatural beings – they used their pain to punch holes in reality. And whatever came through those holes is still there, waiting."

"And now it has Jason and the others," Alice added grimly.

Ethan's phone buzzed. Another anonymous message: "Ward D still hungers. The door still opens. They're waiting for you in Cell 237."

As they packed up the files, neither noticed the shadow that moved independently across the archive room's wall, nor the way the temperature dropped for just a moment. But in the photograph of Dr. Blackburn, still lying on the table, the doctor's face had changed – his smile wider, his eyes completely black.

The truth about Daybridge Max Security was worse than they'd imagined. It wasn't just a hospital. It was a gateway. And somewhere in its sealed lower levels, behind steel doors and silver barriers, something was stirring, awakened by the presence of fresh prey.

Ethan checked his watch. Six hours until sunset. Six hours to prepare for what waited in Daybridge's depths. Whatever horrors lurked in Ward D, whatever entity haunted Cell 237, they were about to learn that a werewolf protecting his pack was equally terrifying.

But as they left the archives, Alice couldn't shake the feeling that somewhere, in the darkness beneath Daybridge Max, something was laughing.

~

CHAPTER FIVE

OFFICIAL CHANNELS

DETECTIVE ALICE CHEN strode through the Paranormal Defense Unit steel and glass headquarters, Ethan close behind. The PDU occupied a deceptively ordinary office building, its true nature hidden behind a façade of government bureaucracy. Unlike other police departments, here the walls were lined with sealed evidence boxes marked with symbols of containment, and officers carried both standard-issue firearms and more exotic weapons.

Captain John Dixon looked up from his desk as they entered, his expression hardening at the sight of Ethan. Silver charms clinked softly on his wrist – standard issue for PDU leadership when dealing with supernatural consultants.

"I wondered when you'd show up, Reeves," Dixon said, closing a file marked "Classification: Omega'. "Three civilians entering a known paranormal hot zone without clearance or backup. This isn't just a missing persons case anymore."

"One of them is my cousin," Ethan replied, his voice tight with controlled anger. "And Ryan Matthews is one of yours."

Dixon's expression shifted slightly. "Ex-PDU. Ryan was discharged after Portland. Medical leave turned into resignation." He pulled out a thick file. "But you're right – this is our jurisdiction. Especially given what we've picked up on our monitoring equipment."

Alice stepped forward. "What kind of readings?"

Dixon activated a holographic display above his desk. Red lines spiked across the graph. "Energy signatures from Daybridge have increased three hundred percent since those kids entered. Whatever's in there is feeding off their presence." He looked directly at Ethan. "And before you do anything stupid, Reeves, you should know – we've lost four agents inside Daybridge Max Security over the years. The last team went in in 2019. We found their equipment three days later. Just their equipment."

"Then give us official backup," Alice argued. "A full PDU team."

"Can't. Won't." Dixon shook his head. "After the 2019 incident, Daybridge Max was classified as a Level 5 containment zone. We maintain the perimeter, monitor for breaches, but direct engagement is prohibited without federal approval."

Ethan's eyes flashed gold. "They could be dying in there."

"They're probably already dead," Dixon said bluntly. "And if they're not, they might be something worse by now. Daybridge Max Security doesn't just kill people, Reeves. It changes them."

He pulled up another file on his screen – security footage from a camera pointed at the hospital. Three figures moved past a window, but their movements were wrong, jerky, inhuman. "This was captured twelve hours ago. Face recognition matched their general profiles, but the biometric readings..." He paused. "They don't register as human anymore."

Alice studied the footage. "Those energy spikes – they're similar to the Portland incident?"

Dixon's face darkened. "Worse. Portland was a single entity using the house as a vessel. Daybridge Max Security is different. Decades of unethical experiments, hundreds of deaths, both natural and supernatural victims. The building isn't just haunted – it's become a nexus point. A wound in reality."

"Then help us close it," Ethan growled.

"You don't close a wound like this," Dixon replied. "You contain it. The PDU's official position is that Daybridge Max Security remains sealed. No rescue attempts. No investigations." He looked at them both. "Unofficially..."

He reached into his desk and pulled out a key card and a small device. "This is Dr. Blackburn's security pass. Still works, according to our intel. And this..." He held up the device. "Prototype reality anchor. Might help stabilize local space-time enough to get you out if things go wrong. But if you take these, this conversation never happened. The PDU will disavow any knowledge. You'll be on your own."

"Not entirely," came a voice from the doorway. They turned to see a tall woman in tactical gear, her right arm marked with ritual scars. "John, you're not sending them in alone."

"Agent Rivera," Dixon sighed. "You're suspended pending review."

"Then I'm acting as a private citizen," Rivera replied, stepping into the office. "Ryan Matthews was my partner for three years. I was there in Portland. I saw what it did to him." She faced Ethan and Alice. "I'm coming with you."

Dixon looked between them, then nodded slowly. "I'll give you a twelve-hour window. After that, the PDU will lock down Daybridge with extreme prejudice. Whatever's inside, whoever's inside... they stay there. Understood?"

Ethan took the key card and device. "Twelve hours."

As they left Dixon's office, Rivera fell into step beside them. "There's something else you should know," she said quietly. "Ryan wasn't just investigating Daybridge Max Security. He was obsessed with cell 237. Said he found references to it in the Portland entity's memories. He believed all these sites were connected – Portland, Daybridge, others. Part of something bigger."

"What was in Portland?" Alice asked.

Rivera's hand unconsciously touched a scar on her neck. "We thought we were dealing with a standard haunting. We were wrong. Ryan... he saw something in that house. Something that showed him the truth about places like Daybridge Max Security. He said they weren't just buildings where bad things happened. They were built to be doorways."

"Doorways to what?" Ethan demanded.

Rivera checked her specialized weapons. "That's what Ryan went to find out. And now we have less than twelve hours to reach him before the PDU seals those doors forever – with us inside or out."

Their phones buzzed simultaneously. The same anonymous number: "The doors swing both ways. But not all who enter remain themselves. Cell 237 remembers you, Agent Rivera. It's been waiting for you to return."

The sun was setting as they left the PDU building. In twelve hours, they would either rescue their people or join them in whatever Daybridge had become. And somewhere in the hospital's depths, behind steel doors and silver barriers, something that had once been Marcus Blackburn smiled with too many teeth, waiting for its guests to arrive.

CHAPTER SIX

DARK OMENS

LILA DARKMAGIC'S sanctum looked different now. Gone were the fairy lights and decorative crystals that once marked her as a novice practitioner. The walls were lined with ancient texts acquired from dubious sources, and symbols of protection glowed faintly in the corners – necessary precautions since her encounter with the Witch Queen last winter had left her changed.

Her fingers traced the silver scar that ran from her left temple to her jaw, a reminder of power that came with a price. The dark magic she'd embraced to save those children had marked her, but it had also opened doors she never knew existed.

"You're sure about this reading?" Ethan asked, studying the cards laid out on her black oak table. Each card had begun smoking slightly when she'd placed it down.

"The cards don't lie," Lila replied, her voice carrying an ethereal echo – another souvenir from her dance with darkness. "But they're afraid, Ethan. Look."

The cards revealed a disturbing pattern: The Tower, The Moon, and The Devil, surrounded by minor arcana that had turned completely black during the reading. In the center, a card she'd never seen before materialized – it showed a hospital corridor with countless doors, and shadows reaching through them.

"The cards have noticed your missing hunters," she continued, her eyes shifting to solid black as she accessed her newer abilities. "But they were never lost. They were invited."

Alice picked up one of the blackened cards, then dropped it as frost spread across her fingers. "Invited by what?"

Lila closed her eyes, drawing sigils in the air that smoldered briefly before fading. "There's an entity there. Old. Patient. It's been collecting for decades, adding to itself, growing stronger. Your ghost hunters..." She paused, her expression troubled. "It wanted their curiosity. Their drive to uncover secrets. It feeds on those qualities."

"Can you help us get them back?" Ethan asked.

Lila opened a cabinet filled with various charms and totems – all significantly darker in nature than her previous collection. "I can give you protection, but I can't enter Daybridge Max Security myself. After the Witch Queen, my magic would resonate too strongly with what lives there. It would sense me immediately."

She handed them each a charm made of twisted black metal and what looked suspiciously like bone. "These will shield you from the lesser entities, the echoes of what was done there. But the thing in Cell 237..." She shuddered. "It's beyond my current abilities to counter."

As she worked on additional protective spells, Lila felt a familiar cold tingle at the base of her skull – a premonition forcing its way through. The vision hit her like a physical blow: Alice, alone in a dark corridor, her flashlight revealing hundreds of doors. A voice calling her name, familiar yet wrong. A choice. A door opening. Then...

Lila gasped, steadying herself against the table. The cards burst into black flame and crumbled to ash.

"What did you see?" Alice asked.

Lila looked at her friend, struggling to keep her voice steady. "Be careful which doors you open, Alice. Some calls shouldn't be answered, even if you recognize the voice." She wanted to say more, to warn her explicitly, but the magic constricted around her throat, preventing the words from forming.

"That's not cryptic at all," Alice said dryly.

Lila began inscribing protective runes on their flashlights and weapons, but her hands trembled slightly. She'd seen what waited for Alice in Daybridge Max Security's corridors. She'd seen the choice her friend would have to make. But most terrifyingly, she'd seen what came after – an empty office at the PDU, a nameplate being removed from a desk, and Ethan standing alone in the rain, holding Alice's badge.

"One last thing," Lila said, pressing a small black crystal into Ethan's hand. "If you hear singing in the lower levels, do not – under any circumstances – follow it. What's down there... it's not human anymore. It hasn't been human for a very long time."

As they prepared to leave, Lila caught Alice's arm. "Whatever happens in there, whatever you hear or see... remember who you are. Promise me."

Alice nodded, though she couldn't fully understand the fear in her friend's eyes. "I promise."

After they left, Lila turned to her mirrors – all twelve of them, arranged in a circle. Each one showed a different angle of Daybridge Max Security in one reflection, a figure that might have once been Dr. Blackburn moved through an endless corridor, opening doors. In another, three distinct shapes huddled in a corner, their forms twisted and wrong. And in the last mirror, Alice stood alone at a crossroads of corridors, reaching for a door handle as a familiar voice called her name.

Lila waved her hand, shattering all twelve mirrors simultaneously. Sometimes seeing the future was a curse. Sometimes knowing what was coming only made it worse.

She began preparing stronger spells. They wouldn't prevent what she'd seen, but perhaps they'd help bring at least some of them home.

The question was: which ones would still be themselves when they returned?

CHAPTER SEVEN

THE ARCHIVIST'S WARNING

Nadia Marsh stood in her study, her fingers trailing over the silver-threaded map of Daybridge when her phone buzzed with Ethan's message about the missing ghost hunters. The pendant at her throat pulsed warmly, a warning she had learned to heed.

"They went into Daybridge Max Security?" She closed her eyes, feeling the wards shift uneasily. "Of course they did."

Her study had evolved since the foundry incident. Ancient texts shared space with modern monitoring equipment. The silver streak in her hair caught the light as she moved to a particular section of her archives, pulling out a leather-bound volume marked "Daybridge Max Security - Ward 13 Anomalies."

When Alice and Ethan arrived, they found her surrounded by open books and glowing ward maps.

"You should have come to me first," Nadia said without looking up. "Daybridge Max Security isn't just another haunted building. It's a breach point."

"A breach point?" Alice asked, eyeing the pulsing lines on Nadia's maps.

"One of fourteen in the city." Nadia pulled up digital overlays showing energy patterns. "But the hospital... it's different. The other sites maintain a balance, but Daybridge..." She gestured to a chart showing spiraling darkness. "It takes. Consumes. The wards there were compromised decades ago by Blackburn's experiments."

Ethan leaned over the maps. "Can you help us get inside?"

"Getting in isn't the problem." Nadia activated a series of crystalline sensors around her study. "It's what happens once you're there. The hospital exists in multiple states simultaneously. Reality is... fluid inside its walls."

She opened her great-great-grandmother's journal. "Elizabeth knew about Blackburn's work. She tried to warn the Council, but they wouldn't listen. Look at this entry from 1925:

"Blackburn has torn holes in the veil between worlds. His experiments haven't just weakened the barriers – they've created something new. An entity that exists between realities, feeding on the pain and fear of its victims. The Council orders containment, but they don't understand. You can't contain something that exists in multiple dimensions at once.'"

The pendant flashed suddenly, and Nadia gasped. Like Lila, she saw fragments of what was coming: Alice in a dark corridor, a choice, a door, an empty desk...

"I can give you ward maps," she said, fighting to keep her voice steady. "Protection charms. But Alice..." She met her friend's eyes. "The hospital remembers everyone who enters. It learns from them. Uses their memories."

"What exactly are we dealing with?" Ethan asked.

Nadia pulled up historical records on her computer. "According to Elizabeth's notes, Blackburn wasn't just experimenting on supernatural beings. He was trying to create doorways between realities. But each experiment left scars in the fabric of space-time. Those scars...

they became something sentient. Something that learned to open its own doors."

She handed them each a crystal that pulsed with silver light. "These are connected to the city's ward network. They'll help you maintain your grip on this reality, but..." She hesitated, looking at Alice. "Be careful what you trust in there. The entity doesn't just create illusions – it recreates memories. Makes them real enough to touch, to follow, to..."

The pendant flashed again, cutting her off before she could reveal too much about Alice's fate.

"There's something else," Nadia said, pulling out a file marked with warning symbols. "Ryan Matthews came to see me two weeks ago. He was researching connections between supernatural sites across the country. He believed Daybridge Max Security was part of a larger pattern – a network of locations where reality had been deliberately weakened."

"Deliberately?" Alice asked. "By whom?"

"He never got to tell me. But he left this." Nadia showed them a photograph of a symbol carved into Daybridge Max Security's foundation. "It's identical to marks found at thirteen other sites across the country. Including Portland."

Ethan studied the symbol. "What does it mean?"

"It's a beacon," Nadia said grimly. "Or an invitation. Ryan believed these sites weren't accidents – they were engineered. Created to allow something to cross over. Something that's been trying to enter our world for a very long time."

She began gathering maps and protective charms. "I can't enter the hospital myself – the wards would react too strongly to my presence now. But I can monitor you from here, try to help you navigate the shifting realities inside."

As they prepared to leave, Nadia caught Alice's arm, just as Lila had done. "Alice... when you reach the lower levels... remember that not all memories should be revisited. Some doors exist only to trap us."

After they left, Nadia turned to her ward maps, watching the silver threads pulse with increasing urgency. The hospital's presence felt stronger, more aware. It was waiting for them.

She opened her own journal and began to write, recording what might be the last normal day in Alice Chen's life. The pendant grew cold against her skin, a reminder that some fates, once glimpsed, could not be prevented – only witnessed and remembered.

In the margins of her journal, she drew the symbol from Daybridge Max Security's foundation. Around it, in Elizabeth's cipher, she wrote: "The doors open both ways. But what comes through may wear familiar faces."

Outside, the wards of Daybridge trembled as something stirred beneath the hospital, sensing new visitors approaching. Something that had worn many faces over the years and would soon wear one more.

~

CHAPTER EIGHT
A TOWN'S VIGIL

THE DAYBRIDGE COMMUNITY Center buzzed with activity as Sonja Miller adjusted the new silver-infused wards around the windows. After last year's incidents, the town's monthly Supernatural Preparedness meetings had evolved from nervous gatherings into well-organized planning sessions.

"Third disappearance this month," Dave Miller, the hardware store owner, said as he distributed the Dave latest batch of protection kits. Each contained iron filings, salt, UV flashlights, and emergency ward markers – standard issue now for Daybridge residents. "And of course, it had to be Daybridge Max."

The older residents shifted uncomfortably at the mention of the facility. They remembered when it was still operational, when ambulances would arrive in the dead of night carrying patients who didn't seem entirely human.

"My grandson works security there," Margaret Wells spoke up from her position at the emergency response table. "Says the ghost hunters' equipment was found scattered across the west parking lot. Recording devices crushed like they'd been thrown from the fourth floor, but no signs of forced entry."

Tom O'Reilly, who ran the local diner, pulled up the town's updated threat assessment map on the large screen. Red markers indicated recent supernatural activity, clustering ominously around Daybridge Max Security Hospital.

"We've had to extend the safety perimeter," he explained, highlighting a new boundary in yellow. "Three delivery drivers reported hearing voices calling them toward the building last week. Thank God they had their ward charms."

The town had changed since accepting its supernatural reality. Wind chimes made of iron and silver hung from most porches. Children wore protection bracelets to school. The neighborhood watch now included "anomaly spotters" trained to recognize signs of supernatural activity.

"At least the PDU's involved now," Officer Jenkins added, adjusting his modified body camera – standard issue since the Witch Queen incident. "Though some folks saw Rivera heading there with Reeves and Detective Chen. Unofficial capacity, from what I hear."

"They're not the only ones interested," said Marcus Wong, the local newspaper editor. He pulled up footage from his phone. "These energy readings were taken yesterday."

The graphs showed massive spikes around the hospital, causing several of the newer residents to gasp. The older ones just nodded grimly – they'd seen this before.

"We need to talk about evacuation protocols," Sonja Miller insisted. "If whatever's in there is getting stronger—"

"It's always been strong," interrupted George Harrison, who'd worked maintenance at Daybridge Max in the sixties. "But it's never been this... active. Something's different this time."

The room grew quiet as Harrison spoke. At eighty-three, he was one of the few left who'd worked at the hospital during its operational years.

"Used to be, it was content to stay inside its walls. But lately?" He shook his head. "The barrier's wearing thin. I can feel it when I drive past – that pull, that whisper. Like it's reaching out."

Rebecca Torres, who ran the town's supernatural alert system, pulled up recent reports. "We've had seventeen incidents in the past week. Shadow figures in windows, electronics malfunctioning, pets refusing to go near the east side of town. And the dreams..."

Several people nodded. The dreams had started after the ghost hunters disappeared – shared visions of endless corridors and doors that opened onto impossible spaces.

"My daughter's class had to relocate," said Linda Park, a local teacher. "The children kept drawing the same thing – a hospital corridor with a figure standing at the end. Always Cell 237."

The emergency response team demonstrated the updated ward configurations they'd established around schools and public buildings. The silver-iron barriers had been reinforced after several residents reported feeling compelled to walk toward the hospital at night.

"We've distributed new emergency kits to all households within a mile of Daybridge Max," Tom Patel, corner store owner reported. "Enhanced warning systems, stronger wards, and direct lines to both the PDU and Nadia Marsh's office."

Sonja Matthews studied the threat map. "If this follows the pattern from Portland, we need to be ready for escalation. The building's influence could expand beyond the current containment zone."

The meeting concluded with updated evacuation routes being distributed and emergency response teams running drills. As residents left, many glanced toward the eastern horizon where Daybridge Max Security Hospital loomed against the darkening sky.

Parents held their children's hands a little tighter, checking their protection charms. Shop owners reinforced their wards. The town's warning system hummed quietly, monitoring for supernatural surges.

Later that evening, at the Daybridge Diner, Tom O'Reilly served coffee to the night shift workers heading to their jobs. Each wore enhanced protection gear – a new normal for a town that had learned to live with its supernatural shadow.

"Stay safe out there," he said, handing them ward-reinforced thermoses. "And remember—"

"Don't answer if someone calls your name," they recited together. "Don't look in the windows. Don't follow the lights."

As they left, Tom glanced at the small shrine by the diner's door – photos of town residents lost to supernatural incidents over the years. He touched his ward charm, silently praying they wouldn't need to add more pictures soon.

But in the distance, Daybridge Max Security Hospital stood silent and waiting, its darkened windows reflecting the setting sun like hundreds of watching eyes. And in Cell 237, something stirred, sensing the town's preparations, their fears, their determination.

It had waited decades. It could wait a little longer.

The town's emergency sirens tested their daily all-clear signal, echoing across Daybridge as residents secured their homes for another night, wondering who else might disappear before this was over.

CHAPTER NINE

PRINT-WORTHY NIGHTMARES

Marcus Wong sat in his office at the Daybridge Chronicle, staring at the blinking cursor on his screen. The draft headline read: "LOCAL PARANORMAL INVESTIGATORS MISSING AT DAYBRIDGE MAX" but his finger hovered over the delete key.

Since taking over the Chronicle five years ago, he'd learned to balance truth with public safety. After the Witch Queen incident, the paper had adopted an unofficial policy: report enough to keep people informed, but not enough to incite panic – or worse, attract thrill-seekers.

"Still wrestling with the story?" Janet Pierce, his senior reporter, leaned against his doorframe. Her camera hung around her neck, containing photos they probably couldn't publish.

"Look at these readings," Marcus said, pulling up the energy graphs on his monitor. The spikes had grown exponentially over the past 48 hours. "The PDU's monitoring equipment hasn't registered levels this high since Portland."

Janet closed the office door. "I interviewed Guard Reynolds. He was on duty when those ghost hunters went in. Says the security feeds showed them reaching Ward C before cutting out. When they came back on..." She handed him a USB drive. "Well, see for yourself."

The footage showed three figures moving through the corridors, but their movements were wrong – jerky, unnatural. They passed beneath a security light, and Marcus froze the frame. Their faces were visible, but distorted, as if something else was wearing their features like ill-fitting masks.

"We can't print this," he said quietly.

"The public has a right to know—"

"The public has a right to sleep at night," Marcus interrupted, remembering the aftermath of the Witch Queen coverage. The tourists it had attracted, the copycats, the additional disappearances. "We print this, every amateur ghost hunter in the Atlantic Northeast will be breaking into Daybridge Max."

He pulled up his draft article:

"SAFETY CONCERNS AT HISTORIC FACILITY

Local authorities advise residents to avoid the Daybridge Maximum Security Hospital grounds following reports of trespassing and structural instability. The PDU (Paranormal Defense Unit) has established an extended security perimeter..."

"That's it?" Janet asked. "Three people are missing, probably dead or worse, and we're running a public safety notice?"

Marcus opened his bottom drawer, removing a thick file labeled "UNPUBLISHED - DAYBRIDGE MAX." Inside were decades of incidents the Chronicle had chosen not to report fully: the missing orderlies in "65, the night guard who walked into Cell Block D and never walked out, the maintenance worker found speaking in tongues about "the thing in Ward F."

"Remember what happened after we ran the full story on the Witch Queen?" he asked. "Three teenage girls tried to recreate the ritual.

Two families moved away. The tourism nearly got more people killed."

Janet sat down heavily. "So we just... what? Pretend nothing's happening?"

Marcus pulled up another document – a more detailed report he'd prepared for the town's emergency response committee. "We inform the people who need to know. We publish enough to keep residents cautious. And we document everything." He gestured to a wall of filing cabinets. "For when it's time."

"When what's time?"

"When whatever's really happening in this town can't be contained by careful reporting anymore."

His phone buzzed – another alert from his monitoring equipment near Daybridge Max. The energy readings had spiked again, accompanied by a photo of strange lights in the upper windows.

Marcus began typing a new draft:

"INCREASED SECURITY MEASURES AT DAYBRIDGE MAX

The PDU has enhanced security protocols around the former maximum security hospital following recent incidents. Residents are reminded that the facility is structurally unsound and legally off-limits to the public. The Daybridge Chronicle encourages citizens to report any unusual activity to local authorities..."

He attached a carefully edited version of the energy readings – enough to warn people away, not enough to attract the curious. At the bottom, he added the standard advisory about keeping protection charms updated and avoiding the eastern part of town after dark.

"The truth is in the subtext," he explained to Janet. "Anyone who needs to understand will read between the lines."

As if to emphasize his point, the lights in his office flickered. His ward charms hummed softly, responding to something that rippled through Daybridge's supernatural fabric.

"There's another story here," Janet insisted. "About Ryan Matthews, the PDU investigation, these energy patterns matching other sites—"

"And we'll document all of it," Marcus assured her. "But right now..." He glanced at his monitoring equipment as another spike registered. "Right now, our job is to keep people safe. Even if that means not telling them everything."

He finished his article, carefully worded to convey urgency without panic. Tomorrow's Chronicle would warn without revealing, inform without inciting. And in his private files, Marcus would continue documenting the real story of Daybridge Max – the missing ghost hunters, the distorted security footage, the things that moved in Ward C when no one should be there.

Because someday, when the time was right or when they had no choice left, the full truth would need to be told. Until then, he'd keep walking the line between information and safety, adding to his files, watching his monitoring equipment, and hoping he was making the right choice.

His ward charms hummed again as another energy spike registered from the direction of Daybridge Max. In the distance, sirens began to wail – not the all-clear signal this time, but something else. Something urgent.

Marcus opened a new document and began to type, recording everything for the history no one was ready to read yet.

CHAPTER TEN

SHADOWS IN THE HALLS

Agent Rivera's modified EMF meter whined as they approached Daybridge Max's west entrance. The security fence, reinforced with PDU containment wards, hummed with residual energy. Beyond it, the building's dark windows seemed to watch their approach.

"Thermal's showing multiple cold spots," Rivera muttered, adjusting her specialized gear. "Moving ones. Third floor, east wing, concentrating around Ward C."

Ethan's eyes glowed faintly gold as he accessed his supernatural senses. "There's something wrong with the shadows here. They're not falling the way they should."

Alice crouched by the scattered equipment near the entrance. A crushed camera, its lens spiderwebbed but memory card intact. A thermal detector torn apart as if by massive force. An EVP recorder, still running, its display showing impossible readings.

"Look at this," she called, pointing her flashlight at marks in the concrete. Three sets of footprints leading in, but they changed about ten feet from the door. The stride patterns became erratic, unnatural, as if the people making them had suddenly forgotten how to walk properly.

Rivera checked her reality anchor – the device Martinez had given them pulsed steadily, creating a small bubble of stable space-time around them. "The barrier's thin here. Be ready for temporal shifts."

They used Blackburn's keycard to enter through a side entrance. The hospital's halls stretched before them, seeming to twist slightly when viewed from the corner of the eye. Their flashlight beams caught dust motes that moved against air currents, forming brief patterns before dispersing.

"Cell block readings are off the charts," Rivera reported, checking her instruments. "Especially—"

"Ward F," Ethan finished. "Yeah. I can feel it. Something in there is... hungry."

Alice's radio crackled. Through the static, they caught fragments: "...please... Cell 237... he's still here... not what we thought..."

"That's Ryan's voice," Rivera said, her hand tightening on her specialized weapon. "But the timestamp... this transmission is from three days ago."

They found more evidence as they proceeded deeper: a phone with its screen cracked in a perfect spiral pattern, playing the same five seconds of video on loop – one of the ghost hunters turning toward something off-camera, their face showing sudden recognition before dissolving into static. A notebook with pages torn out, the remaining ones filled with the same phrase repeated: "The doors remember us all."

"Over here," Ethan called from an intersection of corridors. On the wall, something had been scratched into the paint: "IT WEARS OUR FACES TO MAKE US TRUST IT."

Alice's flashlight beam caught movement at the end of the hall – a figure that seemed to stutter between steps, its movements broken and wrong. Before they could pursue it, it vanished around a corner.

"That was JoJo Lang," Rivera said quietly. "One of the ghost hunters. But..."

"But what?"

"JoJo has a prosthetic left leg. That thing... it had two legs, but it moved like it wasn't sure how many it should have."

Their reality anchor flickered briefly as they passed Ward C. Through the reinforced windows, shadows danced without cast objects, forming shapes that suggested faces, bodies, memories of people who had once walked these halls.

"The PDU files mentioned this," Rivera explained, checking her anchor's readings. "The entity doesn't just take people. It... studies them. Learns from them. Then it uses what it learns to lure others."

Alice's radio crackled again: "Alice... please... I need your help..." The voice was familiar – too familiar. Her own voice, calling from somewhere deeper in the building.

"Don't respond," Rivera warned. "It's learning already. Adapting. Using what it finds in our minds."

They reached another intersection. Each corridor seemed to lead to the same place, despite pointing in different directions. On the wall, a new message had appeared in fresh paint: "WELCOME HOME AGENT RIVERA. PORTLAND MISSES YOU."

Rivera's face went pale. "We need to move. Now. It's not just accessing their memories anymore. It's accessing ours."

As they proceeded deeper into Daybridge Max, the shadows continued their dance, wearing faces they almost recognized, speaking with voices they almost trusted. And somewhere ahead, something waited in Ward F, learning, adapting, preparing to welcome its newest guests.

The reality anchor's light pulsed weaker with each step, as if the very fabric of space was beginning to fray around them. And in the darkness behind them, something followed – something that wore familiar faces and spoke with borrowed voices, patiently waiting for them to make a wrong turn.

CHAPTER ELEVEN
ECHOES OF WARD F

THE STAIRWELL to Ward F felt wrong, each step seeming to hover a millisecond too long beneath their feet. Rivera's reality anchor stuttered, its protective field fluctuating against increasing temporal distortions.

"Dr. Blackburn's office should be ahead," Ethan said, his supernatural senses straining against the building's oppressive energy. "The PDU files mentioned—"

"The files were incomplete," Rivera interrupted, her voice tight. "After Portland, we found evidence that Blackburn never stopped his work. Even after Daybridge Max officially closed, he kept coming back. The PDU tracked his movements until 1987, then... nothing."

They emerged into a corridor lined with observation cells. Each reinforced window showed a different scene playing out in endless loops – moments frozen in time, memories trapped like insects in amber. In one, a patient rocked back and forth, their form flickering between human and something else. In another, orderlies wheeled out a covered gurney that dripped shadows instead of blood.

Alice approached a desk at the nurse's station, its surface covered in patient files that looked far too recent for an abandoned facility. "These dates... some of these are from last year."

"That's impossible," Rivera began, but stopped as her reality anchor gave a warning pulse. The dates on the files were changing as they watched, cycling through different years, different decades.

Ethan moved deeper into the ward, drawn by a familiar energy signature. "There's something else here. Something older than Blackburn's experiments."

They found the doctor's private office at the end of Ward F. The door bore a tarnished nameplate and a symbol that made their ward charms burn cold. Inside, time seemed to move like molasses.

"Look at this," Alice said, pointing her flashlight at a wall of photographs. They showed Blackburn with various "patients" – beings that blurred at the edges, forms that shouldn't exist in three-dimensional space. The photos continued chronologically, well past the hospital's closure, showing the doctor growing older but his eyes becoming younger, hungrier.

Rivera accessed a sealed PDU file on her tablet. "Blackburn wasn't just experimenting on supernatural entities. He was trying to... merge realities. Create spaces where multiple dimensions could overlap."

"He succeeded," Ethan said grimly, his eyes fixed on the last photograph. It showed Blackburn in 1987, standing in this very office. Behind him, something vast and dark seemed to leak through the walls, reaching for him with limbs that existed in too many dimensions at once.

Alice found a journal in the desk drawer, its pages filled with increasingly manic entries:

"The space between realities is populated. They've been waiting for someone to open the doors... The merging process requires anchors – human consciousness to bridge the gap... The ghost hunters will make perfect candidates, their minds already attuned to the supernatural...

She's coming soon. Detective Chen. Her sensitivity to temporal anomalies makes her ideal..."

The writing devolved into symbols that hurt their eyes to look at.

"There," Rivera pointed to a diagram showing Daybridge Max's layout overlaid with mathematical formulas. "Blackburn didn't just experiment here. He turned the entire building into a mechanism – a way to thin the barriers between worlds."

A sound echoed through the ward – footsteps that clicked like dress shoes on linoleum, coming closer with methodical precision.

"Welcome," said a voice they recognized from historical records. "I've been expecting you."

Dr. Blackburn stepped into view at the end of the hall. He looked exactly as he had in the 1987 photograph, but his edges were wrong, as if he was being projected from multiple time periods simultaneously.

"You're not him," Rivera said, her weapon raised. "You're what took him."

The thing wearing Blackburn's face smiled. Behind it, shadows writhed in impossible geometries. "I am what he became. What they all become, eventually. Your ghost hunters understood, in the end. Would you like to see?"

It gestured to a cell across the hall. Through the window, they saw the missing investigators, but wrong – their forms twisted, their movements suggesting extra joints, their faces showing too many angles.

"The merging process requires practice," Not-Blackburn explained. "But I've had so many willing subjects over the years. And now..." It looked at Alice with eyes that reflected other dimensions. "Now you're here. Just as my calculations predicted."

Rivera's reality anchor flared warning red as temporal distortions intensified around them. Through nearby windows, they could see other versions of themselves walking these halls in different times, different realities, all converging on this moment.

"Run," Ethan commanded, his supernatural aura flaring against the encroaching darkness.

As they fled, Blackburn's laughter echoed through Ward F, harmonizing with itself across multiple timelines. Behind them, the thing that had once been a doctor continued its patient work, spreading its influence through the hospital's twisted corridors, waiting for the moment when all realities would finally merge.

And in its wake, shadows danced like memory given form, wearing the faces of everyone who had ever walked these halls, everyone who had thought they could control what lived between worlds, everyone who had become part of something far older and hungrier than they could comprehend.

CHAPTER TWELVE
BETWEEN THE VEILS

THE THING WEARING Blackburn's face flickered, its form splitting into overlapping versions as the hospital's reality fluctuated. Through the distortion, Rivera caught glimpses of the other world bleeding through – a darker reflection of their own, where shadows had substance and time moved like cold honey.

"The Others were right about this place," Not-Blackburn said, its voice echoing from multiple points in space. "Daybridge Max sits precisely where the veils between worlds are thinnest. A perfect door."

Alice's ward charm vibrated violently, responding to the increasing bleed-through between realities. Through the windows, they could see both versions of Daybridge simultaneously – their world and its shadow twin superimposed like double-exposed photographs.

"That's why the ghost hunters came," Ethan realized, his supernatural senses overwhelmed by the dual frequencies of reality. "They weren't investigating hauntings. They were tracking convergence points."

Rivera pulled up classified PDU files on her tablet. "Portland was just the beginning. These weak spots are appearing across the country, following a pattern. But here..." She gestured to the hospital's twisted corridors. "This is where it started. Where they first began pushing through."

Not-Blackburn's smile stretched too wide. "The Others have waited so long, watching through these thin places. Learning. Adapting. Preparing for the final merger."

Through gaps in local space-time, they caught glimpses of vast shapes moving in the other world – beings of shadow and concept that defied three-dimensional geometry. The Others, ancient and patient, reaching through the weakening barrier between realities.

"My experiments," Not-Blackburn continued, "were merely preparation. Making this place ready. And now..." It gestured to where the ghost hunters' transformed bodies hung suspended between worlds, existing in both realities simultaneously. "Now we begin the true work."

Alice's radio crackled with voices from both worlds – dispatchers reporting reality breaches across Daybridge, the ward network straining against increasing pressure from the other side. In the distance, sirens wailed in two different frequencies.

"The PDU's been wrong all along," Rivera said, checking readings that showed both worlds' energy signatures merging. "We thought we were dealing with isolated supernatural incidents. But it's all connected. Every haunting, every anomaly, every breach – they're all part of their plan."

Through the hospital's windows, they could see two versions of Daybridge overlapping more completely with each passing moment. In the shadow world, dark figures moved through familiar streets, wearing forms that almost resembled humanity. The Others, preparing to cross over.

"You're too late to stop it," Not-Blackburn said, its form now fully straddling both realities. "The doors are opening. The barriers are falling. Soon, both worlds will be one again, as they were always meant to be."

Ethan's supernatural aura flared as he sensed something massive stirring in the space between worlds. "We need to go. Now. Whatever's coming through—"

"Has already begun," Not-Blackburn finished. The walls around them rippled as local reality buckled under increasing pressure from the other side. "The Others are done waiting. This is their time. Their world. We were just keeping it warm for them."

As they ran from Ward F, the hospital groaned with the weight of two realities pressing against each other. Through every window and doorway, they could see both versions of the world splitting and reforming, the barriers between dimensions growing thinner with each passing moment.

Their reality anchor sparked and died, overwhelmed by the conflicting frequencies of overlapping worlds. And in the darkness behind them, something vast and ancient pushed through the weakening veil between realities, bringing with it the promise of a world where shadows ruled and humanity was nothing but a fading memory.

Rivera's tablet displayed final readings before shorting out: convergence points activating across the city, the ward network failing, and a message from PDU headquarters that chilled them to their cores:

"MULTIPLE BREACHES DETECTED. DIMENSIONAL COLLAPSE IMMINENT. THE OTHERS ARE HERE."

In both worlds, Daybridge trembled on the edge of transformation, waiting to see which reality would prevail.

CHAPTER THIRTEEN

LOST BETWEEN WORLDS

"SHE WAS RIGHT HERE," Ethan's voice cracked as he swept his flashlight across the empty corridor where Alice had stood moments before. Only her dropped flashlight remained, rolling gently back and forth between realities, its beam cutting through both versions of the hospital simultaneously.

Rivera checked her failing equipment. "The temporal readings are off the scale. Whatever happened, she's—" She stopped, realizing what the data suggested. "She's not gone. She's everywhere."

The corridor stretched before them, existing in both worlds at once. In their reality, it was decay and abandonment. In the other, it writhed with living shadows. Alice's voice echoed from multiple points in space-time:

"Ethan... I can see... everything. All the versions. All the times. They're all happening at once."

His supernatural senses strained as he tried to locate her. Each time he thought he caught her signature, it slipped away, scattered across multiple dimensions. Through nearby windows, he glimpsed her walking these halls in different times, different realities – sometimes solid, sometimes translucent, sometimes something in between.

"The Others are using her as an anchor," Not-Blackburn's voice drifted from everywhere and nowhere. "Such perfect sensitivity to temporal fluctuations. She's helping us merge the worlds, whether she wants to or not."

Ethan's hands clenched, his aura flaring gold with barely contained power. "Where is she?"

"Here. There. Everywhere the barriers are thin. Would you like to see?"

The walls rippled, showing them glimpses through dimensional tears: Alice in Ward C, her form flickering between states of existence. Alice in the basement, walking paths that existed in both worlds. Alice in places that shouldn't exist at all, where reality folded in on itself like a möbius strip.

"My god," Rivera breathed, watching the readings spike. "She's becoming a convergence point. Her consciousness is spreading across multiple realities, creating new weak spots."

Through the dimensional bleeding, they heard Alice's voice again, overlapping with itself: "There's something else here... something older than the Others... it's been waiting... using Blackburn... using all of us..."

Ethan moved deeper into the hospital's twisted geometry, following traces of Alice's scattered consciousness. Each step took him through layers of overlapping reality – past, present, and possible futures bleeding together.

"The PDU files," Rivera said, following close behind. "There was a theory about consciousness acting as a bridge between dimensions. If Alice's mind is spread across multiple realities—"

"Then we can use that connection to find her," Ethan finished. His supernatural senses expanded, searching for the unique frequency of Alice's consciousness among the chaos of merging worlds.

They found her belongings scattered through both realities – her notebook in their world, its pages filled with warnings. Her badge in the shadow world, its surface crawling with living darkness. Her voice, growing more distorted with each echo:

"They're showing me... everything. The hospital... it's not just a building... it's a machine... designed to... oh God, Ethan, don't let them—"

Static overwhelmed her words as reality buckled around them. Not-Blackburn's laughter resonated through both worlds: "She understands now. Soon, you will too."

Ethan's aura pulsed as he pushed his abilities to their limit, trying to lock onto Alice's scattered consciousness. Through tears in space-time, he caught glimpses of her fighting against the merger, trying to hold onto her singular existence as the Others pulled her across dimensions.

"There!" He pointed to where the realities overlapped most strongly. For a moment, Alice's form solidified, her eyes meeting his across the dimensional divide. She pressed her hand against the barrier between worlds, leaving prints in both realities simultaneously.

"Don't," she warned, her voice clearer for a moment. "It's what they want. They need you to—"

She fractured again, her consciousness scattered across multiple points in space-time. The Others moved through the shadows around them, their ancient patience finally wearing thin as the barriers continued to weaken.

"Agent Rivera," Ethan's voice was tight with controlled fury. "Get back to the PDU. Tell them what's happening. I'm going after her."

"That's suicide," Rivera protested. "The dimensional instability—"

"Will tear me apart? Good. Maybe then I can exist in multiple realities too. Maybe then I can reach her."

Before Rivera could stop him, Ethan strode toward the point where the worlds overlapped most strongly. His supernatural aura blazed as he forced his consciousness to expand, to exist in multiple dimensions like Alice.

The hospital groaned around them as another set of barriers fell. And somewhere in the spaces between realities, Alice's voice echoed with a final warning:

"Ethan, the Others aren't the enemy. They're running from something worse. Something that's been here all along, wearing Blackburn's face, wearing all our faces, waiting for the worlds to—"

Static consumed her words as reality fractured again. And in the darkness between dimensions, something ancient and patient watched as its carefully laid plans finally began to bear fruit.

CHAPTER FOURTEEN

CRITICAL CONTAINMENT

THE PDU's mobile command center hummed with activity, its specialized equipment struggling to process the cascading reality breaches across Daybridge. Captain John Dixon stood before a wall of monitors, each displaying different temporal anomalies bleeding through the city's ward network.

"Status report," he demanded, watching as another section of the map turned red.

"Multiple time signatures overlapping downtown," Agent Sarah Rodriguez responded, her hands flying over holographic displays. "We're getting readings from 1987, 2024, and... dates that don't exist yet. The temporal bleeding is accelerating."

Through the command center's reinforced windows, Daybridge flickered like a faulty television signal. Buildings shifted between past and present states. Streets rearranged themselves according to decades-old city plans. Citizens reported seeing themselves walking to work hours before they'd left home.

"Containment Team Alpha reports Ward F is completely compromised," another agent called out. "They're seeing multiple versions of the ghost hunters' disappearance playing out simultaneously. The hospital exists in at least three different time periods at once."

Rodriguez's tablet buzzed with an urgent message from Rivera: "ALICE CHEN COMPROMISED. DIMENSIONAL SCATTER. BLACKBURN WAS WORKING WITH THEM. THE OTHERS ARE COMING THROUGH."

"Sir," Rodriguez's voice cracked. "Look at these pattern analyses."

The main screen displayed overlapping temporal signatures. What had appeared to be random anomalies now formed a clear design – a massive clock face laid over Daybridge, with Daybridge Max at its center. Time wasn't just bleeding through; it was being deliberately manipulated.

"They're not just breaking through space," Rodriguez realized. "They're breaking through time. Using our own history against us."

Reports flooded in from across the city:

A coffee shop where customers aged decades between sips

A park where children played eternal games of tag, their forms ghostly and translucent

An intersection where traffic lights cycled through patterns from every year since their installation

A neighborhood where houses existed in all their previous states simultaneously

"Timeline integrity at 47% and falling," Rodriguez reported. "The temporal anchors aren't holding. We're getting bleed-through from—" She stopped, staring at his readings. "From timelines that never happened. Possibilities that were prevented. They're all becoming real."

Rodriguez watched as multiple versions of reality competed for dominance across Daybridge. Through quantum viewers, she could see the Others moving through the weakened spots, their ancient forms distorting time itself as they pushed through.

"New signal from Detective Chen," an analyst called out. "It's... fragmented across multiple timestreams."

Alice's voice played through the command center's speakers, each word coming from a different point in time:

"The hospital... is a clock... Blackburn built it... to synchronize... all the times... when they... break through..."

"Sir!" Rodriguez's hands shook as she pulled up new data. "The temporal anomalies – they're not random. They're following the same pattern as Portland but amplified. It's like..."

"Like they're learning from their failures," Captain Dixon finished. "Each breach teaches them more about manipulating our timeline."

She accessed classified files about the Portland incident, seeing it with new understanding. It hadn't been a failed attempt at breaking through – it had been a test run. Practice for Daybridge.

The command center's temporal shielding groaned as another wave of distortions washed over the city. Through the windows, they could see multiple versions of Daybridge overlaid on each other – the past, present, and possible futures bleeding together.

"Timeline integrity at 35%," Rodriguez reported. "We're losing cohesion. The Others are using the temporal instability to—"

He vanished mid-sentence, replaced by a version of himself from three hours ago, then one from next week, then back to now. The effect rippled through the command center as reality struggled to maintain consistency.

Rodriguez's secure line crackled with Ethan's voice: "Alice is scattered across multiple timestreams. I'm going in after her. But there's something else you need to know – something worse than the Others. Check the original Daybridge Max blueprints. The whole building is a temporal focusing lens. Blackburn didn't just build a hospital. He built a—"

Static consumed his words as another temporal wave hit. Outside, the sky flickered between day and night, dawn and dusk, as time itself began to unravel.

"New priority," Dixon commanded. "Forget containing the breaches. Focus on stabilizing the timeline around the hospital. Whatever's coming through, whatever Blackburn built that place to be – we need to make sure there's still a Daybridge left when it arrives."

The command center hummed with renewed activity as the PDU fought to hold reality together. But through their quantum viewers, they could see the truth: time wasn't breaking down.

It was being broken down. Deliberately. Systematically. By something that had been planning this moment since before Daybridge Max was built.

And in the spaces between seconds, in the moments between moments, the Others continued their relentless advance – not as invaders, Dixon now realized, but as refugees, fleeing something that had finally found its way to our world through the cracks in time itself.

CHAPTER FIFTEEN

ECHOES OF YESTERDAY

Sonja Miller watched her daughter play in the backyard – all three versions of her daughter, to be exact. Eight-year-old Emily chased her six-year-old self while her ten-year-old version sat in the oak tree, legs dangling through time itself. Sarah had stopped trying to determine which Emily was "real" two days ago.

"Mom," all three called in unison, "when's dinner?"

"Which dinner?" she whispered to herself, noting how the kitchen window showed both morning light and evening shadows simultaneously.

Down on Baker Street, Tom Patel stood behind the counter of his convenience store, watching customers from different decades browse the shelves. A teenager in modern clothes reached for an energy drink while his father's younger self, wearing 90s fashion, grabbed the same drink thirty years earlier. Their hands passed through each other, neither aware of the other's existence.

"Price check on aisle three," the intercom announced in Tom's voice – yesterday's voice, today's voice, and tomorrow's voice overlapping.

At Daybridge Elementary, Principal Blanche Watson faced a unique crisis. The morning assembly featured students from every year since the school's founding in 1962. The fire marshal would have had concerns about overcrowding if the children weren't partially phased through each other, their morning pledges creating an echo that spanned generations.

"I've called three sets of parents about their child's behavior," she told her secretary. "Unfortunately, they were all the same child, just from different months."

The Daybridge Diner became a temporal hub where citizens sought some semblance of normalcy, even as they sat in booths that existed in multiple decades at once. Martha O'Reilly, the owner's grandmother, served coffee alongside his granddaughter Jennifer, both the same age now thanks to timeline bleed.

"The special today is meatloaf," they announced together. "It was also the special yesterday, and tomorrow, and thirty years ago."

In the park, elderly George Peters sat on his favorite bench, watching his younger self propose to his late wife Helen. The scene had been playing out every afternoon since the temporal shifts began. Sometimes Helen said yes, sometimes no, sometimes the words came out in reverse. George couldn't decide which version hurt more to watch.

"The hospital," he muttered to himself, to his younger self, to no one at all. "It all started when they built that damned hospital."

At the First National Bank, teller Lisa Wang tried to explain to a frustrated customer why their account showed transactions from 1995 mixing with current deposits. Through the window, she could see three different versions of Main Street – one with horse-drawn carriages, one with modern cars, one with vehicles she didn't recognize yet.

The Daybridge Gazette's latest headline read: "TEMPORAL ANOMALIES CONTINUE - Yesterday's Paper Available Tomorrow." Editor Marcus Wong had given up trying to maintain publication dates when his computer began displaying articles that hadn't been written yet alongside ones from decades past.

At St. Mary's Church, Father Timothy conducted services for congregations from multiple eras, his sermons echoing across time itself. Some parishioners swore they could see themselves attending their own funerals.

"Even prayer feels different now," he confided to a visitor. "When I speak to God, I hear answers from past and future prayers all at once."

The Daybridge Police Department's dispatch center was overwhelmed with calls:

"My son is playing with himself as a child..."

"I just watched my house being built around me..."

"There's a family having dinner in my living room, but it's not my family..."

"I keep getting mail delivered from next year..."

Officer Danny Martins sat in his patrol car, watching traffic violations that hadn't happened yet and accidents that would never occur. His radar gun showed speeds from different decades simultaneously.

In her flower shop, elderly Rose Milligan arranged bouquets with blooms from different seasons – spring daffodils next to summer roses next to autumn chrysanthemums, all fresh, all existing at once. She'd stopped checking delivery dates when she received an order she wouldn't place until next week.

"Time was simpler when I was young," she told a customer who might or might not exist yet. "Of course, I'm young right now too, somewhere in the city."

At the high school football field, Coach Burke watched his team practice against themselves from last season, the players' forms overlapping as they ran plays that spanned months. The scoreboard displayed every score from every game ever played, all somehow adding up to both victory and defeat.

And through it all, Daybridge Max loomed on its hill, existing in all its states at once – under construction, fully operational, abandoned, and something else, something that hadn't happened yet but was somehow bleeding backward through time.

The citizens of Daybridge adapted as best they could. They learned to check multiple watches, to greet themselves in passing, to accept that memory and prophecy had become the same thing. They developed new social etiquette for temporal encounters and tried not to think too hard about which version of reality was "real."

But in quiet moments, when the timelines briefly aligned and clarity returned, they all felt it – the sensation of something massive approaching through the cracks in reality, something that had turned their city into a temporal maze for its own unfathomable purpose.

And in every time, in every version of Daybridge, people looked toward the hospital on the hill and whispered the same question:

"What happens when it finally arrives?"

CHAPTER SIXTEEN

THE AWAKENING HOUR

IN THE TWILIGHT DISTRICT, realities didn't just bleed – they hemorrhaged. Ancient beings watched with a mixture of terror and opportunity as time itself became malleable.

At the Crimson Crown, Alexi Volkov's usual clientele of vampires existed in multiple stages of their unlives simultaneously. Elder vampires watched their past selves make deals and forge alliances, while future versions whispered warnings that distorted in temporal static.

"The Others aren't the true threat," a centuries-old vampire told his decade-younger self. "They're running from something that makes us look like children playing at immortality."

In the Wild Court, the fae were nearly mad with excitement and fear. Their innate connection to chaos made them particularly sensitive to the temporal distortions. Queen Maeve's court danced between moments, their revels splitting and reforming across multiple timelines.

"The veils are thinning," Maeve observed, her form shifting between all her aspects at once – maiden, mother, crone, and something older still. "But not just between worlds. Between whens."

The werewolf packs gathered in Hangman's Woods, where multiple moons hung in the sky – past, present, and futures that hadn't happened yet. Alpha **Fenris** prowled between timestreams, scenting changes in reality itself.

"The moon," he growled to his assembled packs, "it shows us what's coming. All the moons do. The hunt that ends all hunts approaches."

In the Witch's Quarter, covens struggled to maintain their temporal anchors as their magic responded to multiple versions of reality. Spells cast now affected the past, while enchantments from decades ago suddenly activated.

Miranda Thornheart's warren of prophecy expanded exponentially, showing not just possible futures but all futures, all pasts, all moments bleeding together. Her seers babbled in tongues that wouldn't exist for centuries.

"The hospital," they chanted in unison, "it calls to the deep places. The old ones stir. What sleeps beneath time itself awakens."

At the Crossroads Market, where supernatural beings had traded in secrets and power for generations, merchants found their wares existing in multiple states of transaction simultaneously. Deals made centuries ago revised themselves. Future bargains cast shadows into the present.

The shadow-folk were perhaps the most affected, their natural ability to slip between spaces now extending to slipping between times. They reported strange movements in the deep darkness between moments – things that had always been there, watching, waiting for time itself to weaken enough for their emergence.

In forgotten subway tunnels beneath the city, the Tunnel Tribes – those supernatural beings who had rejected surface society – gathered in council. Their shamans painted warnings on walls that existed in multiple eras at once:

"THE WALLS OF TIME GROW THIN

THE DEEP ONES WAKE

WHAT WAS BURIED RISES

WHAT WAS CHAINED BREAKS FREE"

But not all supernatural beings viewed the temporal crisis with dread. Some saw opportunity.

"Think of it," a young vampire lord argued in the Crimson Crown's back room. "With time in flux, we could undo the treaties. Return to the old ways, before the PDU, before human law bound us."

"Fool," his elder self responded from three decades hence. "You don't understand what's coming. This isn't our chance to rule – it's our chance to survive."

In her winter court, Maeve gathered her most trusted advisers – beings who remembered the world before time flowed in one direction, before reality settled into rigid patterns.

"The humans think this is about invasion," she told them, her voice echoing across multiple whens. "The Others, breaking through. But they're wrong. This is about restoration. What was sundered long ago seeks to become whole."

The werewolf packs marked territorial boundaries that shifted through decades. The witch covens wove spells that existed in all times at once. The shadow-folk slipped between moments, gathering intelligence about what approached through the cracks in reality.

In the depths of Hangman's Woods, where the oldest trees remembered times before human feet walked these lands, supernatural beings of all factions gathered in secret council.

"We have choices to make," Maeve addressed them, her form flickering between all her aspects. "When time itself breaks, when what comes through reshapes reality – do we fight to preserve this world, with its human laws and PDU oversight? Or do we welcome the change, return to deeper, darker magics?"

The gathered beings shifted uneasily, watching shadows that moved between seconds and hearing whispers that came from no single when.

"Choose quickly," Alexei advised, his vampire's senses detecting something massive approaching through the temporal distortions. "What sleeps beneath Daybridge Max is awakening. What Blackburn called forth is almost here. And when it arrives..."

He left the sentence unfinished, but they all felt it – the sensation of ancient power stirring, of something vast and patient finally reaching the moment it had planned for since before time flowed in orderly lines.

In every supernatural enclave across Daybridge, in every moment that existed simultaneously, beings of power and shadow watched the hospital on the hill and made their choices. Some prepared for war. Some prepared for submission. Some prepared to run.

And in the spaces between moments, in the darkness between times, something older than supernatural, older than natural, continued its patient work of unraveling reality itself.

CHAPTER SEVENTEEN

THE GREAT SUNDERING

IN THE DEPTHS of Daybridge Max's temporal nexus, Alice's scattered consciousness accessed memories that weren't her own – glimpses of history older than time itself, when reality was whole and undivided.

Before the Sundering, there was one world. A place where what humans called "natural" and "supernatural" existed in perfect balance. Physical and ethereal, material and spiritual, light and shadow – all aspects of the same unified existence. The Others weren't others at all, but part of the great whole.

Then came the Great Fear.

Through the temporal bleeding, Alice witnessed fragments of that ancient catastrophe:

Something stirred in the deep places of unified reality. Something that devoured consciousness itself, that fed on awareness and identity. The ancients called it the Void-Between-Thoughts, a cancer in the fabric of existence that threatened to consume all awareness.

In desperation, the ancient beings – those who would become the Others – attempted a desperate gambit. They would split reality itself, creating a barrier between physical and spiritual existence. This divide would contain the Void-Between-Thoughts, trapping it in the spaces between worlds.

The Sundering was catastrophic. Reality tore apart like a sheet of cosmic fabric, creating two separate but parallel worlds. In one, physical laws dominated – the world of humanity and linear time. In the other, consciousness and possibility ruled – the shadow realm of the Others.

But the division was never meant to be permanent.

"The worlds are like magnets," Not-Blackburn's voice echoed through multiple timelines. "Opposing forces that naturally seek to reunite. What was sundered wants to be whole."

Through her temporally scattered awareness, Alice understood more:

The Others hadn't fled to their shadow realm – they had sacrificed themselves, becoming guardians of the barrier, keeping the Void-Between-Thoughts contained. For eons they watched humanity develop in the physical world, unable to warn them of what lurked in the spaces between realities.

But the Void-Between-Thoughts was patient. It worked slowly, subtly, weakening the barriers between worlds. It whispered to humans through dreams, inspiring them to build structures that would serve as convergence points – places like Daybridge Max, designed to focus and amplify the natural resonance between separated realities.

"Blackburn wasn't working for us," the Others communicated through the temporal static. "He was influenced by it. The hospital isn't a door for our return – it's a cage being unlocked."

The truth became clear: The Others weren't invading; they were trying to prevent the worlds from reuniting too quickly, too catastrophically. Each intrusion into the physical world was an attempt to reinforce the weakening barriers, to prevent total collapse.

But if the worlds did reunite...

Alice's consciousness expanded across possible futures:

In one timeline, the reunion was gradual, controlled. Physical and spiritual reality slowly reintegrated, restoring the natural balance that existed before the Sundering. Humanity evolved to comprehend and exist in a fuller, richer version of reality.

In another, the reunion was violent and sudden. The shock of unfiltered spiritual energy overwhelmed human consciousness. The Void-Between-Thoughts, freed from its prison between worlds, began its ancient feast anew.

And in the most terrible possibility, the reunion created something worse – a twisted hybrid reality where the Void-Between-Thoughts ruled supreme, using the merged worlds as a breeding ground for horrors that defied comprehension in any single reality.

Through the temporal chaos, the Others sent their warning:

"The worlds must reunite – this is inevitable and necessary. But it must happen slowly, carefully, with preparation and purpose. What your people call supernatural activity – these are pressure valves, controlled releases of building tension between realities."

"Blackburn's machine," they continued, "disrupts this delicate process. It forces convergence too quickly, too completely. And in doing so, it weakens our ability to contain what lurks between worlds."

Alice understood finally: The Others weren't the enemy. The real threat was what they had sacrificed everything to contain – the Void-Between-Thoughts that waited in the spaces between realities, that had influenced Blackburn to build its perfect trap, that even now worked to devour consciousness itself.

The hospital's temporal nexus pulsed with possibility as multiple versions of reality competed for dominance. In every timeline, in every possibility, one truth remained constant: The worlds were reuniting. The only question was whether it would happen on humanity's terms, the Others' terms, or something far worse.

And in the spaces between moments, between thoughts themselves, ancient hunger stirred as barriers weakened and the time of feeding drew near.

Through the temporal static, Alice broadcast her understanding to Ethan, to the PDU, to anyone who could still perceive truth through the chaos of merging realities:

"We're not fighting against invasion. We're fighting for controlled integration. The Others aren't our enemy – they're our only hope of surviving what comes next."

In the hospital's deepest subbasement, in a room that existed in all times simultaneously, something ancient smiled with Blackburn's borrowed face and continued its patient work of unraveling reality itself.

CHAPTER EIGHTEEN

THE HIDDEN PAGE

NADIA MARSH'S fingers trembled as she handled the fragile manuscript, its pages yellowed and brittle with age. The PDU archives, normally her sanctuary of order and knowledge, felt different tonight. The temporal distortions had reached even this carefully warded space, causing the dates on file cabinets to shift and change, documents appearing and disappearing as time itself fluctuated.

She had found the text buried in a section that shouldn't have existed – a shelf that appeared only when viewed from certain angles, in certain moments between moments. The manuscript's cover bore no title, only a symbol she recognized from the hospital's original blueprints: a circle split by a jagged line, with an eye watching from the divide.

"Recording begins," she spoke into her archival device. "Time... uncertain. Multiple temporal signatures detected. Document appears to predate known history. Language shifts between recognizable forms and... something older."

The pages seemed to resist traditional chronology, their contents changing depending on when she read them. But slowly, carefully, she began to piece together the narrative:

Before the Division of Forms

When Shadow and Substance Were One

When Thought and Matter Danced as Equals

There Came the Great Devouring...

"This can't be right," Nadia muttered, cross-referencing with other texts that flickered in and out of existence around her. But as she read further, patterns emerged, connections formed:

The manuscript spoke of a time when reality was whole, when what humanity now called "supernatural" was simply natural. It described beings of pure consciousness existing alongside physical matter, thought and form intertwined in perfect harmony.

Then came passages that made her blood run cold:

It Feeds on Awareness

It Consumes Identity

It Hollows What Is Full

It Empties What Is Whole

The Void Between Thoughts Grows Hungry...

"Cross-reference with File PDU-777-B," she commanded her system. "Keywords: void, consciousness, ancient threats."

The archives hummed around her as time-shifted documents aligned themselves. On her desk, papers from different eras organized themselves into patterns, forming connections across centuries:

A monk's account from 1247 describing "the empty spaces between thoughts"

A witch hunter's diary warning of "that which devours awareness"

A PDU field report from 1962 noting "anomalous consciousness readings in subjects near Daybridge Max"

Her hands shaking, Nadia continued reading the ancient text:

The Sundering Was Necessity

The Division Was Survival

Two Worlds from One

A Barrier of Separation

To Trap What Hungers...

"They did it on purpose," she whispered, understanding dawning. "The Others – they didn't choose to leave. They chose to guard..."

The manuscript's pages turned themselves, showing her diagrams that seemed to move and shift: reality splitting like a cell dividing, but with something trapped in the membrane between. The Others, accepting their role as guardians, keeping the Void-Between-Thoughts contained in the space between worlds.

A note appeared in the margin, written in Blackburn's hand but dated decades before his birth:

"The hospital must be built. The alignment must be perfect. When the time comes, the spaces between thoughts will need their feast..."

Nadia's archival device sparked as temporal energy surged through the room. Around her, the very history she had dedicated her life to cataloging began to unravel and rewrite itself. Through the archive's high windows, she could see multiple versions of Daybridge existing simultaneously.

The manuscript's final pages showed her what would happen if the worlds reunited too quickly, too catastrophically:

The Void Grows Strong

Through Cracks in Time and Thought

When Walls Between Worlds Fail

The Great Feast Begins...

"Emergency archival update," she spoke into her device, her voice steady despite her fear. "The Others are not invaders. Repeat: the Others are not invading our world. They're trying to prevent something worse. The hospital – Blackburn's design – it's not just connecting worlds. It's releasing what they imprisoned themselves to contain."

The lights flickered as another temporal wave passed through the archives. Documents from future centuries appeared on her desk, their warnings written in languages that didn't exist yet. The manuscript's pages turned by themselves, showing her glimpses of possibilities:

A future where the worlds slowly, carefully reunited, healing the ancient sundering under controlled conditions

A future where sudden reunification shattered human consciousness, leaving empty shells where people used to be

A future where the Void-Between-Thoughts ruled both worlds, consciousness itself becoming extinct

In the margins of these possible futures, she noticed something else: equations, calculations, architectural drawings. Blackburn's notes, scattered across time, showing how each element of the hospital's design served to weaken the barriers between worlds.

"He knew," she realized. "He didn't design Daybridge Max as a hospital. He designed it as a door. But not for the Others to come through..."

The manuscript's final page shifted between multiple versions, but the warning remained constant:

What Was Sundered Seeks Union

What Was Trapped Seeks Freedom

In The Space Between Thoughts

The Void Grows Hungry...

Nadia gathered her findings, preparing to deliver them to PDU command. But as she stood, she noticed one last note appearing on her desk – written in her own hand, but dated three days from now:

"Too late. It's already awake. The hospital was never meant to keep things out. It was meant to let something in. Something that's been waiting, wearing familiar faces, patient beyond time itself..."

The lights flickered again, and in the darkness between moments, Nadia Marsh, PDU Archivist, finally understood what all her careful cataloging had been leading toward. The true history she had discovered wasn't about the Others at all.

It was about what came before them, what they had sacrificed everything to contain, and what was finally, after eons of patience, about to break free.

CHAPTER NINETEEN
WHISPERS IN THE DARK

ETHAN'S ENHANCED hearing had always been both a gift and a curse, but in Daybridge Max, it became something else entirely – a window into impossible conversations. Standing in the hospital's east wing, he could hear whispers that existed in multiple times at once, voices that spoke in languages that hadn't existed yet or had been dead for millennia.

"Status check," he subvocalized into his PDU comm unit, trying to ground himself in protocol. "Does anyone else pick up these frequencies?"

Static answered him – or rather, multiple versions of static, each carrying fragments of different realities' radio chatter.

The whispers grew louder as he approached Room 437:

...the door opens both ways...

...he built it to see between...

...all times are one time here...

His enhanced senses detected subtle changes in air pressure, electro-magnetic fluctuations that shouldn't be possible. The walls themselves seemed to pulse with temporal energy, existing in multiple states simultaneously.

"Hey, Detective Chen," he started to say, but caught himself – Alice was scattered across timestreams now, her consciousness fragmented between moments. He was alone here, trying to make sense of what Blackburn had really built.

A child's laughter echoed down the corridor, but wrong – played backward and forward simultaneously, coming from everywhere and nowhere. His enhanced vision caught movement in his peripheral view: shadows that moved independent of light sources, forms that existed between moments of time.

...the hunger grows...

...spaces between thoughts...

...wear their faces, speak their words...

The whispers were becoming clearer, more coherent. Ethan's training kicked in as he documented each anomaly:

Voices speaking from within solid walls

Temperature fluctuations that followed mathematical patterns

Light bending around corners that shouldn't exist

The smell of ozone and something older, something that predated scent itself

He reached the nurse's station, where monitors displayed vital signs from patients who hadn't been admitted yet and who had been discharged decades ago. The readings overlapped, creating patterns that looked disturbingly intentional.

"This wasn't just experiments," he realized aloud. "The whole hospital – it's some kind of..."...lens between worlds...

...focus point for the rejoining...

...hunger older than time...

His enhanced senses picked up new details: The floor plan wasn't just architecturally sound – it was mathematically precise in ways that served no medical purpose. The placement of every room, every corridor, every piece of equipment formed patterns that only became apparent when viewed across multiple timelines simultaneously.

The whispers grew more insistent:

...Blackburn knew...

...built it for us...

...no, built it for IT...

...the space between your thoughts...

Ethan's hand went to his service weapon, though he knew it would be useless against whatever was speaking. His enhanced hearing picked up conversations from other times:

Doctors discussing patients who hadn't been born yet

Nurses reporting deaths that hadn't happened

Blackburn himself, his voice echoing from decades past: "The design is perfect. When it wakes, it will have everything it needs..."

The lights flickered – not from electrical failure, but from reality itself struggling to maintain coherence. Through the windows, Ethan could see multiple versions of Daybridge existing simultaneously, the city's timeline fracturing around the hospital like waves breaking against a stone.

...we tried to warn you...

...trapped between worlds...

...but now it wakes...

His enhanced vision caught movement in a nearby room. Through the window, he saw Blackburn – not the historical figure, but something wearing his form, existing in all times at once. It turned to look at him, and its eyes...

Ethan's enhanced senses shut down automatically, a survival reflex triggered by something his consciousness refused to process. When they came back online seconds later, he understood with horrible clarity:

"The experiments weren't the point," he transmitted to PDU command. "The hospital itself is the experiment. Blackburn didn't build it to study supernatural phenomena. He built it to create them. Or to let something through that..."

The whispers rose to a crescendo:

...space between thoughts...

...void that hungers...

...wearing faces, stealing time...

...finally, finally, finally...

The hospital's temporal bleeding intensified. Through his enhanced senses, Ethan perceived layers of reality peeling away like old wallpaper, revealing something that existed in the spaces between moments, between thoughts themselves. Something that had been waiting, patient beyond time, for all the pieces to align.

The whispers spoke as one now, using all voices from all times:

OPENING

And in that moment, Ethan's enhanced senses showed him the truth: Daybridge Max hadn't been built as a hospital at all. It was something much older, wearing the shape of medical science, designed by something wearing Blackburn's face, all to create this perfect moment when the spaces between thoughts grew wide enough for ancient hunger to feed once more.

Through the temporal static, he sent one final message to PDU command:

"It's not coming through from their world to ours. It's already here, in the spaces between. And Blackburn... Blackburn was never really Blackburn at all."

The whispers laughed in frequencies that existed between sounds, and the void between thoughts grew wider, wider, wider...

CHAPTER TWENTY

THE HIDDEN LABORATORY

THE TEMPORAL DISTORTIONS led Ethan to a section of Daybridge Max that shouldn't exist – a space between the hospital's official floors, accessible only when time shifted just right. The corridor lights flickered between decades: stark fluorescent, warm incandescent, and something else that cast shadows in impossible directions.

His enhanced senses picked up the lingering scents of fear, antiseptic, and ozone – layered across multiple timelines like geological strata. The walls bore scratches from both human and inhuman hands, some made decades ago, some yet to be made.

"Found something," he subvocalized into his comm. "Subbasement level, between moments. Blackburn's private lab."

The security keypad beside the reinforced door displayed different codes depending on when he looked at it. Ethan watched the numbers shift through time until he saw the pattern – not a code, but a mathematical sequence that described the space between seconds.

Inside, the laboratory existed in multiple states simultaneously:

Clean and operational, machines humming with power

Abandoned and dusty, equipment draped in sheets

Actively used, with fresh samples and running experiments

Something else, a state of existence that human language couldn't describe

"Alice," he whispered, seeing her name on charts and files scattered across time. "What did he do to you?"

The lab tables held equipment that defied conventional medical purpose:

Devices for measuring consciousness itself

Machines that recorded thoughts as wavelengths

Temporal resonance chambers

Something that looked like an MRI scanner but designed to image the spaces between thoughts

Ethan's enhanced vision caught movement in the shadows – memories of experiments playing out across multiple timelines:

Blackburn, speaking to someone off-camera: "The human mind creates gaps between thoughts. Spaces. Empty places that something else can... occupy."

Alice strapped to a table, her consciousness being systematically fragmented: "I can see them... between the moments... they're not what we thought..."

The doctor's journal entries scattered across decades:

Day 147: Subject shows remarkable adaptive capabilities. Consciousness remains coherent even when distributed across multiple timestreams.

Day 258: The Others are not the true focus. They're merely symptoms of a larger phenomenon. What exists in the spaces between...

Day 365: Chen's unique mental architecture makes her the perfect candidate. Her detective's mind, combined with supernatural sensitivity... she'll be able to perceive IT when the time comes.

Ethan's hand trembled as he picked up a file labeled "Project Looking Glass." Inside, he found:

Alice's complete psychological profile

Detailed maps of her neural patterns

Notes on her supernatural sensitivity

Calculations showing how her consciousness could be used as a lens to view something that existed between moments of time

"She wasn't a victim," he realized with growing horror. "She was a prototype."

The lab's deeper reaches held more disturbing discoveries:

Chambers designed to fragment consciousness across multiple timestreams

Devices for widening the gaps between thoughts

Specimens of... something... preserved in temporal stasis

A wall of photographs showing the same subjects existing in multiple times simultaneously

A video monitor flickered to life, showing Blackburn in his final recorded entry:

"The hospital was never meant to be a barrier," the doctor's image said, his face occasionally shifting into something else. "It's a lens, focusing reality itself through the prismatic awareness of human consciousness. And Chen... Chen is the perfect observer. When she sees IT, when she finally comprehends what exists in the void between thoughts, she'll open the way for..."

The recording degraded into temporal static, but Ethan's enhanced hearing picked up whispers beneath the noise:

...wearing his face...

...using his hands...

...building our door...

...feeding time approaches...

In the center of the lab, he found what looked like a diagnostic chair surrounded by temporal measurement equipment. Alice's name was on the readout display, but the dates... the dates showed she was still here, would always be here, had never been here at all.

"Command," Ethan transmitted, his voice steady despite his growing dread. "Blackburn wasn't studying supernatural phenomena. He was creating them. The experiments, the hospital, Alice... it's all connected. He needed a consciousness that could perceive across timestreams, that could see into the spaces between thoughts. He needed..."

His voice trailed off as he saw the final piece of evidence: a series of brain scans showing consciousness itself being systematically hollowed out, creating spaces for something else to occupy.

And on the wall, written in Blackburn's hand but dated decades after his death:

"The void between thoughts grows hungry. Alice sees. Alice understands. Alice opens the way."

The temporal distortions intensified around him as Ethan finally understood what the doctor – or whatever had been wearing the doctor's face – had actually built: not just a hospital, not just a laboratory, but a machine for widening the spaces between thoughts until something ancient could squeeze through.

The lights flickered one final time, and in that moment of darkness, Ethan heard Alice's voice from all times at once:

"I see it now. I see what lives between the thoughts. And it sees us too."

Behind him, in the depths of the laboratory that shouldn't exist, something stirred in the spaces between moments, patient beyond time, wearing faces that had never truly been their own.

CHAPTER TWENTY-ONE

THE FINAL THRESHOLD

THE TEMPORAL BLEEDING reached its peak as Ethan stood in Blackburn's hidden laboratory, reality fracturing around him like broken glass. His enhanced senses detected movement in spaces that shouldn't exist – something vast and ancient, unfolding from the void between thoughts.

...finally... finally... finally...

The whispers came from everywhere and nowhere, speaking in voices stolen from across time. The thing wearing Blackburn's face stepped out of a shadow that bent in impossible directions, its form flickering between identities like static on an old TV.

"You're too late, Detective Reeves," it said in multiple voices simultaneously. "The spaces are wide enough now. She sees us. Through her eyes, we see everything."

Alice's fragmented consciousness swirled around them like quantum smoke, existing in all times at once. Ethan's werewolf senses picked up her distress, her awareness scattered across countless moments.

"Let her go," Ethan growled, feeling the wolf rise within him. His transformation rippled across multiple timelines – he was human, wolf, and something in between, all at once.

The entity laughed in frequencies that hurt to hear. "Let her go? She's our lens, our perfect observer. Through her detective's mind, her supernatural sensitivity, we finally have the perspective we need to... feed."

Ethan's enhanced vision saw the truth beneath Blackburn's stolen face – something that existed in the empty spaces between thoughts, ancient beyond time, patient beyond measure. It had worn many faces, built many doors, all leading to this moment.

The wolf in him understood instinctively what human language couldn't describe: This wasn't just a fight for Alice, or for the hospital. This was a battle for consciousness itself.

"You've worn masks for too long," Ethan snarled, his voice resonating across multiple frequencies. "Time to see what you really are."

He launched himself at the entity, his werewolf form shifting between states of existence. His claws, enhanced by supernatural strength and temporal resonance, tore through layers of reality.

The thing that wasn't Blackburn responded with impossible geometries, its form expanding to fill the spaces between seconds. Tentacles of void-stuff whipped through time itself, trying to find the empty spaces in Ethan's consciousness.

But a werewolf's mind worked differently – instinct and intellect, human and wolf, leaving no gaps for the void to exploit.

"Interesting," the entity hissed through borrowed mouths. "Your kind always was... resilient. But can you protect her?"

Alice's scattered consciousness swirled faster, being pulled into the spaces between thoughts. Ethan could hear her across multiple timelines:

"I see it... I see everything... the void... so hungry..."

Ethan's enhanced senses worked overtime, processing information from all realities simultaneously:

The hospital's true nature as a lens for focusing consciousness

The entity's patient plan across centuries

The Others' desperate attempt to prevent this moment

Alice's unique mind being used as the final key

He fought with everything he had:

Claws that could rend time itself

Strength enhanced by supernatural fury

Senses that could track prey across dimensions

A mind that existed in perfect harmony with its animal nature

The entity struck back with weapons older than thought:

Void-tentacles that sought to hollow out consciousness

Temporal shockwaves that disrupted reality

Whispers that could shatter sanity

The weight of eons of patient hunger

But Ethan had one advantage the ancient entity hadn't counted on: He wasn't fighting alone.

Deep in the fragmented spaces of her consciousness, Alice began to resist. Her detective's mind, scattered across time, started making connections:

"The spaces between thoughts... they're not empty at all... they're full of... us..."

The entity faltered, its borrowed faces showing genuine concern for the first time in eons. "No... you're meant to observe, to open the way..."

Ethan pressed his advantage, his werewolf form moving through multiple moments simultaneously, striking at the entity's true nature beneath its masks. His claws found purchase in something that existed between realities.

"You hide in the spaces between thoughts," he growled, "but you forgot what fills those spaces – imagination, creativity, the connections that make us who we are!"

Alice's consciousness began to reintegrate, her scattered awareness turning from lens to weapon. "I see you now... really see you... you're not vast at all... you're empty..."

The entity thrashed in temporal agony as its true nature was exposed – not an ancient god, but a parasite that fed on the fears that lived between thoughts. It had waited so long, worn so many faces, built so many doors...

"Now!" Ethan roared across all timelines.

Alice's consciousness snapped back into focus, her detective's mind and supernatural sensitivity working in perfect harmony. The spaces between thoughts slammed shut, trapping the entity in a prison of awareness.

The laboratory twisted through impossible geometries as reality tried to reassert itself. Ethan stood his ground, his werewolf form anchored in multiple moments, holding the entity as it thrashed and screamed in frequencies that existed between sound.

"This isn't over," it howled through disintegrating borrowed faces. "The void between thoughts will always hunger..."

"Maybe," Ethan answered, human and wolf speaking as one. "But those spaces belong to us. They're filled with all the things you tried to devour – hope, love, imagination. The connections between thoughts are our strength, not our weakness."

The temporal bleeding began to stabilize. Alice's consciousness fully reintegrated, her mind stronger for having seen across time. The entity's stolen faces melted away, leaving only the truth – a parasite that had finally run out of places to hide.

In the end, it wasn't Ethan's supernatural strength or Alice's unique mind that won the day. It was the realization that the spaces between thoughts weren't empty at all – they were filled with everything that made consciousness worthwhile.

As reality settled back into its proper flow, Ethan held Alice's newly solid form, both of them watching as the thing that had worn so many faces finally faded into true emptiness, its ancient hunger finally, finally satisfied.

The hospital's walls still whispered, but now they spoke of victory, of consciousness preserved, of thoughts connected rather than divided. And in the spaces between those whispers, there was only the sound of life itself, flowing ever onward through time's eternal stream.

∼

CHAPTER TWENTY-TWO

THROUGH THE LENS OF SHATTERED TIME

ETHAN FOUND Alice in a room that existed in all moments simultaneously – a temporal nexus where Blackburn's experiments had fragmented her consciousness across multiple timelines. She sat in the diagnostic chair, her awareness scattered like light through a broken prism, experiencing all possible versions of reality at once.

"Ethan," she spoke in overlapping voices, each from a different moment in time. "I see everything now. All the pieces. What he really was. What he was building toward."

Her eyes shifted colors as different timelines bled through her perception – brown, blue, green, and sometimes colors that shouldn't exist. The temporal displacement had transformed her detective's mind into something both more and less than human.

"Take it slow," Ethan said, his enhanced senses struggling to process her fractured state. "What did you see?"

"Blackburn was never Blackburn," she began, her words echoing across multiple frequencies. "It wore his face, used his hands, built this place across decades of patient work. But the real Blackburn... the real one died long ago, in spaces between thoughts."

Images flickered around her like temporal static:

The real Blackburn discovering something in the void between consciousness

The entity taking his form, continuing his work

The hospital being built to exact mathematical specifications

Experiments designed not to study supernatural phenomena, but to create them

"The hospital," Alice continued, her consciousness sliding between moments, "it's not just a building. It's a lens, focusing reality itself. Every room, every corridor calculated to create the perfect conditions for... for..."

Her words fractured as memories from multiple timelines competed for space:

"It lives in the spaces between thoughts," she explained, her voice shifting between octaves. "The gaps in consciousness where one idea ends, and another begins. It's been there all along, patient beyond time, wearing faces, building doors, waiting for the right moment to..."

Temporal feedback surged through the room. Through Alice's fractured perception, Ethan saw:

The true purpose of Blackburn's experiments

The entity's patient plan across centuries

The Others' desperate attempts to prevent this moment

The hospital's role as a focusing lens for consciousness itself

"The experiments weren't about studying supernatural phenomena," Alice's overlapping voices revealed. "They were about creating the perfect observer. Someone who could see across time, whose mind could comprehend the spaces between thoughts. Someone who could... who could..."

"Could what?" Ethan pressed, fighting the vertigo of multiple timelines.

"Could see IT," she whispered in all voices at once. "Really see it. Give it form through observation. Make it real."

Her fractured consciousness projected understanding directly into Ethan's mind:

The entity had waited eons, wearing stolen faces, conducting experiments across time. It needed a specific type of mind – one that combined supernatural sensitivity with analytical thinking. A detective's mind enhanced by exposure to the paranormal.

"My disappearance wasn't random," Alice continued, temporal tears streaming down her cheeks. "It chose me. Prepared me. Fragmented my consciousness across time until I could perceive the spaces between thoughts. Until I could see..."

Her words cut off as another surge of temporal energy pulsed through the room. Through her shattered perception, Ethan witnessed the entity's true plan:

Using the hospital as a lens to focus reality

Using Alice's mind as the perfect observer

Using observation itself to give form to formless hunger

Using the spaces between thoughts to birth something ancient into modern reality

"But it made a mistake," Alice said, her consciousness beginning to reintegrate. "It showed me too much. I see what it really is now. What it's always been. And I see how to..."

The air crackled with temporal energy as something responded to her growing awareness. Shadows that existed between moments began to move with purpose.

"We don't have much time," Alice warned, her consciousness almost whole again. "It's coming. What lives in the spaces between thoughts.

What wore Blackburn's face. What built this place as its perfect trap. And now that I can see it..."

"It can see through you," Ethan finished, understanding dawning.

Alice nodded across multiple timelines simultaneously. "The hospital isn't haunted, Ethan. It was built to be a haunting. Every detail designed to create the perfect conditions for something older than time to..."

The lights flickered as reality struggled to maintain coherence. Through the windows, they could see multiple versions of Daybridge existing simultaneously, the city's timeline fracturing around the hospital like waves breaking against a stone.

"It's starting," Alice whispered, her newly reintegrated consciousness blazing with terrible understanding. "The spaces between thoughts are getting wider. The void is getting hungry. And now that I can see it clearly..."

The shadows between moments deepened as something ancient stirred, patient beyond measure, wearing faces that had never truly been its own. Through Alice's enhanced perception, through Ethan's supernatural senses, they both finally understood what Blackburn – the real Blackburn – had discovered in the spaces between thoughts.

And in those spaces, in the gaps between one moment and the next, between one thought and another, ancient hunger prepared to feast on consciousness itself.

"We have to end this," Alice said, standing on legs that existed in multiple timelines. "Before it uses what it learned from my mind. Before it widens the spaces between all thoughts. Before it..."

The entity that wasn't Blackburn stepped out of a shadow that shouldn't exist, wearing a smile that had never been human.

"Before I what, Detective Chen?" it asked in voices stolen from across time. "Before I thank you for seeing so clearly? For finally giving form to formless hunger?"

The void between thoughts grew wider, wider, wider...

CHAPTER TWENTY-THREE

THE HEART OF DARKNESS

REALITY FRACTURED like breaking glass as Ethan, Alice, and the thing wearing Blackburn's face converged in the hospital's temporal nexus – a space that existed in all times simultaneously. The walls pulsed with otherworldly energy, decades of carefully calculated architectural geometry finally achieving its true purpose.

"Beautiful, isn't it?" the entity said through Blackburn's borrowed mouth. "A machine built to widen the spaces between thoughts. And now, thanks to Detective Chen's perfect observation, those spaces are finally wide enough for..."

The void between moments yawned open, revealing something ancient and hungry that had waited patiently behind borrowed faces and stolen names.

"The ghost hunters," Ethan growled, his werewolf form shifting between states of existence. "They weren't just victims, were they? They were test subjects."

"Of course," the entity smiled with too many teeth. "Each investigation, each encounter with the supernatural, widening the gaps in their consciousness. Creating space for... awareness."

Through his enhanced senses, Ethan perceived the truth:

Ryan Matthews' EMF readings detecting temporal bleeding

JoJo Lang's psychic sensitivity being systematically amplified her cameras capturing impossible moments between moments

Jason Reeves' protective wards failing by mathematical design

"You led them here," Alice realized, her fractured consciousness perceiving across multiple timelines. "Every haunting, every supernatural event – it was all orchestrated to bring them to this point."

The entity's form rippled, Blackburn's face momentarily revealing something that existed between shapes. "We needed to understand human consciousness, its limits, its breaking points. Each investigation brought us closer to perfecting our approach. And now…"

The hospital's geometry began to align, every room and corridor focusing reality like a lens. Through the windows, they could see multiple versions of Daybridge existing simultaneously as time itself began to unravel.

Ethan's wolf nature surged forward, understanding on an instinctual level what had to be done. "Alice, the ghost hunters – their consciousness, it's still here, isn't it? Trapped in the spaces between thoughts?"

She nodded across multiple timelines. "Not just trapped. Connected. The entity didn't just study them. It linked them. Used their combined awareness to…"

"To create the perfect observers," the thing wearing Blackburn's face finished. "A network of consciousness, all perceiving the spaces between thoughts. All giving form to formless hunger."

The battle erupted across multiple planes of existence:

Ethan attacked with supernatural fury:

Claws that could tear through temporal fabric

Strength enhanced by primal rage

Senses that could track prey across dimensions

A mind unified between human and wolf

The entity responded with weapons older than time:

Void-tentacles that sought to hollow out consciousness

Reality-warping geometries

Whispers that could shatter sanity

The weight of eons of patient hunger

Alice, her detective's mind spread across multiple timelines, saw the pattern:

"The ghost hunters – they're not just victims. They're part of the geometry. Their consciousness forms the final points of the pattern!"

"The hospital isn't just a building," Alice called out as reality buckled around them. "It's a machine for focusing consciousness itself. And we're all part of the equation!"

The entity laughed in frequencies that hurt to hear. "Finally, you understand. Every investigation, every encounter, every moment of awareness – all building toward this perfect convergence of consciousness."

But Ethan saw something the ancient entity had missed. Through his enhanced senses, through Alice's fractured perception, through the combined awareness of the ghost hunters, he understood:

"You made us observe you," he growled. "But you forgot – observation goes both ways."

Alice's consciousness, linked to the ghost hunters through the entity's own design, began to pulse with purpose:

Ryan's scientific precision

JoJo's psychic insight

Jason's protective knowledge

"The spaces between thoughts," Alice said, her voice resonating across all timelines, "they're not empty at all. They're filled with everything you tried to devour. And now we see you. Really see you."

The entity's stolen faces began to crack as the combined consciousness of its victims turned observation into weapon. The hospital's carefully calculated geometry became a prison rather than a lens.

"You've worn masks for too long," Ethan snarled, attacking with supernatural fury enhanced by unified awareness. "Time to see what you really are."

The thing that wasn't Blackburn thrashed in temporal agony as its true nature was exposed – not an ancient god, but a parasite that had waited in the spaces between thoughts, wearing borrowed faces, building doors across time.

"Even if you destroy this form," it howled through disintegrating masks, "the void between thoughts will always hunger!"

"Maybe," Alice answered, her consciousness joined with the ghost hunters in perfect clarity. "But those spaces belong to us. They're filled with connection, imagination, hope – everything you tried to hollow out."

The hospital's geometry shifted one final time as reality reasserted itself. The ghost hunters' trapped consciousness began to reintegrate, their combined awareness turning from the entity's lens into its cage.

In the end, it wasn't Ethan's supernatural strength or Alice's unique mind that won the day. It was the realization that consciousness itself – with all its gaps and spaces and connections – was stronger than ancient hunger.

The entity that had worn so many faces finally dissolved into true emptiness; its patient plan undone by the very awareness it had tried to exploit. The hospital's dark purpose was transformed, its calculated geometry now containing rather than focusing.

As the temporal bleeding subsided, Ethan held Alice while the ghost hunters' consciousness returned to their bodies. The walls still whispered, but now they spoke of victory, of minds connected rather than hollowed, of thoughts flowing freely through spaces that belonged, finally and forever, to the living.

The hospital's secrets were revealed at last – not as a story of supernatural evil, but as a testament to the strength of united consciousness against the patient hunger that lived in the spaces between thoughts.

And in those spaces, now and forever, there was only the sound of minds thinking, dreaming, imagining – filling the void with everything that made consciousness worth protecting.

CHAPTER TWENTY-FOUR

THE PRICE OF SEEING

DAWN BROKE over Daybridge Max in multiple shades of possibility, reality still settling back into its proper flow after the temporal chaos. Ethan and Alice sat on the hospital's roof, watching as the last traces of dimensional bleeding faded from the sky.

"The headaches still haven't stopped," Alice said softly, her consciousness newly reintegrated but forever changed. "I keep seeing... echoes. Moments that haven't happened yet, or happened differently, or might never happen at all."

Ethan nodded, his enhanced senses still picking up traces of temporal distortion. "The wolf feels it too. Like the world is slightly out of sync, everything vibrating at frequencies that shouldn't exist."

The city below them existed in singular time again, but they both knew things would never be truly normal. Their encounter with the entity had left permanent marks on their perception. For Alice, fragments of scattered consciousness refused to fully realign, leaving her with the ability to perceive gaps between thoughts. Memories from multiple timelines competed for space in her mind, a detective's intuition forever altered by impossible knowledge.

Ethan's enhanced senses had become attuned to temporal bleeding, the wolf's awareness now extending to things that existed between moments. His instincts operated across multiple possibilities, and he bore scars from wounds inflicted outside of normal time.

"The ghost hunters," Alice began, her voice carrying echoes of other conversations from other timelines. "They're recovering, but..."

"But they'll never be the same," Ethan finished. "None of us will."

They had visited their former colleagues in the recovery ward. Ryan Matthew's instruments now detected frequencies that shouldn't exist. JoJo's psychic abilities had been permanently amplified. Jason Reeves's protective wards had evolved to account for temporal threats.

"We stopped it," Alice said, watching reality ripple like heat waves around the hospital's architecture. "But there are others out there, aren't there? More things hiding in the spaces between thoughts?"

Ethan's wolf nature stirred, sensing ancient hungers that still lurked in dimensional shadows. "The entity wasn't alone. It was just the first to figure out how to wear human faces, how to build doors between moments."

The morning air carried whispers of other possibilities – more hospitals built to impossible geometries, more beings watching from the gaps in consciousness, more patient hunters waiting in the void between thoughts. The battles were far from over.

"We know what to look for now," Alice said, her fractured perception scanning across multiple timelines. "The patterns, the signs, the mathematical precision of engineered hauntings."

"And we're not the same people they thought they could use," Ethan added, feeling the wolf's strength flow through multiple possibilities simultaneously.

They had paid a price for their victory. Nights were filled with dreams from other timelines, and reality sometimes seemed to slip sideways. The constant awareness of what existed between thoughts weighed heavily upon them, along with the burden of impossible knowledge.

But they had gained something too. Their understanding of consciousness itself had deepened, and they could now perceive threats across multiple dimensions. They drew strength from unified awareness, and most importantly, they had each other, bound by shared impossible experiences.

"The PDU will need to adapt," Alice said, her detective's mind already analyzing future possibilities. "New protocols for temporal incursions, training for dimensional bleeding, ways to detect consciousness-based threats."

"We'll need to train others," Ethan agreed, his enhanced senses detecting more subtle distortions in reality. "Build a network of people who can see between moments, who can protect the spaces between thoughts."

They stood together at the edge of the roof, watching the city wake to a world that was both more and less than it had been before.

"It won't be easy," Alice said, her consciousness flickering briefly across multiple possibilities. "Teaching others to see without breaking them, to understand without losing themselves."

"No," Ethan agreed, the wolf in him alert to ancient hungers still waiting in dimensional shadows. "But we have something they don't."

"What's that?"

"Each other. Connection. The very thing they try to hollow out of consciousness."

The morning light strengthened, pushing back the last traces of temporal bleeding. Below them, Daybridge Max stood as both warning and fortress – its geometry now turned against the very forces it had been built to serve.

They had survived, but survival came with responsibility. They would guard the spaces between thoughts, protect those who couldn't see the threats, and train a new generation of defenders. Most importantly, they would remember what lived in the void, patient and hungry.

"Ready?" Ethan asked, offering his hand across multiple possibilities.

Alice took it, her consciousness stable despite the echoes of other time-lines. "Ready. The darkness isn't finished with our world."

"No," he agreed, feeling the wolf's strength flow through their connection. "But neither are we."

Together they descended from the roof, changed but unbroken, carrying the weight of impossible knowledge and the strength of unified purpose. The world might never know how close it had come to being hollowed out, but they would remember.

And in the spaces between thoughts, in the gaps between moments, they would stand guard against the patient hunters that waited in dimensional shadows, protecting the very thing that made consciousness precious – the connections that filled the void with light.

The sun rose fully over Daybridge, a single timeline reasserting itself, but Ethan and Alice knew better now. They had seen behind reality's curtain, and they would never stop watching, never stop fighting, never stop protecting the spaces between thoughts from the ancient hungers that waited there.

The price of seeing was high, but the cost of looking away would be infinitely higher.

Together, they walked into a future that existed in multiple possibilities, ready to face whatever emerged from the spaces between thoughts, carrying the light of connected consciousness against the patient dark.

CHAPTER TWENTY-FIVE

PRINT AND SHADOW

THE CURSOR BLINKED ACCUSINGLY on Marcus Wong's screen as he stared
at the half-written article. Three weeks after the Daybridge Max incident, and he still couldn't find the right words to describe what had
happened – or what hadn't happened, depending on which version of
reality one believed.

"Local Ghost Hunters Return with Missing Memories"

No. Delete. Too sensational.

"Paranormal Investigation at Historic Hospital Ends in Mystery"

Better, but still not quite right.

His coffee had gone cold, the newsroom around him oddly quiet for a
Tuesday afternoon. Ever since that night at the hospital, ordinary
sounds seemed muffled, as if reality itself was holding its breath. Or
maybe that was just him, still trying to process the gaps in his own
memory.

JoJo Lang sat across from his desk, her hands wrapped around her
own untouched coffee. The former lead investigator of Daybridge
Paranormal looked different now – older somehow, though not in any

way he could precisely define. The EMF meter on her belt occasionally chirped at frequencies that shouldn't exist.

"Take it from the beginning," he prompted, hitting record on his phone. "What do you remember?"

"We entered the hospital at 8:42 PM," JoJo began, her voice steady but distant. "Standard protocol. Ryan had the cameras, Jason was setting up protective wards, and I was taking baseline readings. Everything normal until..."

She trailed off, frowning at something invisible. The EMF meter chirped again.

"Until?"

"There's just... static after that. Like trying to remember a dream while you're still dreaming it." She pressed her fingers to her temples. "The next clear memory is waking up in the recovery ward three days later."

Marcus made a note, trying to ignore the way his pen seemed to leave afterimages on the paper. Agent Rivera had told a similar story yester-day, though her cameras had somehow captured impossible images – photographs of moments that existed between moments, all of them unusable for publication.

Jason Reeves had been even less help, his usually precise knowledge of protective wards now scattered and transformed. He spoke of geometric patterns that hurt to look at, of mathematics that operated outside normal space-time.

"The official report mentions temporal anomalies," Marcus said, watching JoJo's's reaction carefully. "And Detective Chen's statement references "reality distortions.' Can you elaborate?"

"You feel it too, don't you, Marcus?" JoJo looked at him intently. "The way time doesn't quite flow right anymore. The way memories seem to overlap, like multiple exposures on the same film."

She was right. Ever since that night, he'd been experiencing strange echoes in his reporting. Stories seemed to write themselves in multiple versions simultaneously. Sources remembered events that hadn't happened yet, or had happened differently.

"Detective Reeves and Detective Chen declined to comment for this article," he said, changing the subject. "But hospital records show they were present during the... incident."

"Ethan and Alice," JoJo murmured, then blinked as if surprised by her own familiarity with their names. "They... they were there. I think. There are moments when I almost remember..."

The EMF meter squealed, its display showing impossible readings. JoJo switched it off with practiced ease, but her hands were shaking slightly.

"What about the missing time?" he pressed. "Three days unaccounted for, and yet medical examinations show no signs of trauma or injury."

"No physical trauma," JoJo corrected. "But our instruments... they're different now. They detect things they shouldn't be able to detect. And sometimes, late at night, I think I remember..."

She stopped again, struggling with memories that seemed to exist just out of reach. Marcus understood the feeling. His own notes from that night made less sense with each reading, the words somehow shifting between drafts.

"The hospital itself seems unchanged," he offered. "I did a walk-through last week. No sign of the geometric anomalies mentioned in the initial reports."

"Unchanged to normal perception, maybe," JoJo said cryptically. "But try looking at it through a camera lens, or an EMF reader, or... or the spaces between thoughts."

The phrase sent an unexpected chill down his spine. In his research for this article, he'd found references to "spaces between thoughts" in multiple witness statements, though none could explain exactly what they meant.

"How do you want me to write this, JoJo?" he asked finally. "What's the story people need to hear?"

She was quiet for a long moment, the afternoon light through his office window casting strange shadows across her face. "Write that we went in as investigators and came out as witnesses. Write that some mysteries can't be solved, only survived. Write that reality is... flexible, and that sometimes the gaps in memory are protective rather than problematic."

"And the truth?"

"The truth?" JoJo smiled sadly. "The truth is writing itself in frequencies we can't quite hear, in moments we can't quite remember, in spaces we can't quite see. Write what you can, Marcus. The rest... the rest lives in the static between stations, in the blur between frames, in the silence between words."

He looked down at his notes, trying to find a narrative thread among the temporal contradictions and missing memories. How does one tell a story about events that exist in multiple versions simultaneously? How does one report on truths that hide in the spaces between facts?

In the end, his article ran on page three of the Sunday edition:

"PARANORMAL INVESTIGATION RAISES MORE QUESTIONS THAN ANSWERS

By Marcus Wong

Three weeks after their mysterious disappearance and equally mysterious return, the members of Daybridge Paranormal continue to recover from their experience at Daybridge Max Hospital. While official reports cite temporal anomalies and reality distortions, the exact nature of events remains unclear..."

It wasn't the whole truth. It couldn't be. But as he filed the story and powered down his computer, Marcus realized that maybe some truths weren't meant to be fully told. Maybe some stories lived best in the gaps between what could be said and what could never quite be remembered.

The EMF meter on JoJo's belt chirped one final time as she left his office, detecting frequencies that shouldn't exist in a world that wasn't quite the same as it had been before. And somewhere in the spaces between thoughts, between moments, between words, the real story continued to write itself in a language none of them could fully understand.

CHAPTER TWENTY-SIX
RECALIBRATION

RYAN MATTHEWS SET his modified EMF meter on the conference table, where it hummed at frequencies that shouldn't exist. Around the table, the remnants of Daybridge Paranormal gathered for their first case meeting since the hospital incident. The basement office of their headquarters felt different now – closer somehow, as if the walls existed in multiple locations simultaneously.

"First order of business," Ryan began, his voice steady despite the temporal echo that followed each word. "We need to establish new protocols. Our old methods..."

"Are obsolete," JoJo finished, adjusting her camera strap. The device had been recording continuously since Daybridge Max, capturing images that existed between conventional frames. "Look at this."

She spread photographs across the table. To an ordinary observer, they would appear blank or blurred. But to their altered perceptions, each image revealed layers of reality bleeding into one another. Moments stretched and compressed, consciousness leaving traces like light trails in a long exposure.

Jason stood at the whiteboard, drawing protective sigils that followed non-Euclidean geometries. His understanding of wards had evolved beyond traditional boundaries. "The mathematics are different now," he explained, sketching patterns that seemed to move when viewed peripherally. "Protection isn't just about space anymore. It's about protecting the spaces between thoughts."

Their newest case file lay unopened in the center of the table. A local restaurant, nothing special at first glance. Complaints of time distortions – meals arriving before being ordered, conversations repeating with subtle variations, customers experiencing memories of meals they hadn't eaten yet.

"Six months ago, we would have dismissed this as imagination," Ryan said, opening the file. "Now..."

"Now we know better," JoJo added, studying her latest photographs. "Look at the temporal bleeding around the building's foundations. The architecture is starting to fold in on itself."

Jason stepped back from his diagrams, which had begun to pulse with their own inner rhythm. "The question isn't whether something's happening there. It's whether we're ready to face it with our new... perspectives."

Jason's EMF meter chirped a pattern that matched the pulse of Jason's sigils. He had modified the device after their recovery, adapting it to detect distortions in consciousness as well as electromagnetic fields. The readings from the restaurant showed familiar patterns – reality thinning around the edges, time flowing in multiple directions simultaneously.

"We're not the same team we were before," Jason acknowledged, touching the scar at his temple where memories of multiple timelines had left their mark. "Our equipment has evolved. Our understanding has expanded. But most importantly..."

"We know what we're really looking at now," JoJo finished, her photographer's eye-catching moments between moments. "The paranormal was never about ghosts or spirits. It was about consciousness itself, about the spaces where reality becomes... permeable."

Jason added a final curve to his protective geometry, creating a pattern that seemed to breathe. "The restaurant case. Standard investigation protocol would have us looking for EMF spikes, temperature variations, physical evidence. But now..."

"Now we look for the gaps," Ryan said. "The places where thoughts don't quite connect. The moments that exist in multiple versions. The geometries that shouldn't be possible."

They had developed new tools since their recovery:

JoJo's cameras had been modified to capture temporal bleeding, their shutters operating between conventional moments. Jason's wards incorporated mathematical principles that operated outside normal space-time. Ryan's instruments detected fluctuations in consciousness itself, measuring the thickness of reality at any given point.

"We go in tomorrow night," Ryan decided, his altered perception already mapping possible timelines. "Full spectrum monitoring, but not just of the physical space. We need to measure the gaps between customers' thoughts, the places where memory doesn't quite align with reality."

"I've developed new wards," Jason said, gesturing to his diagrams. "They don't just protect space anymore. They protect consciousness itself, maintain temporal stability in unstable zones."

JoJo held up her camera, its lens reflecting light that hadn't happened yet. "And I'll document everything – not just what happens, but what might have happened, what's happening in other versions, what exists between the moments of happening."

The EMF meter's rhythm synchronized with the pulse of Jason's wards and the temporal bleeding in JoJo's photographs. Their experiences at Daybridge Max had changed them, but they had adapted, evolved. They understood now that the paranormal wasn't about hunting ghosts – it was about investigating the very nature of consciousness and reality.

"Remember," Ryan said as they packed their equipment, "we're not just investigators anymore. We're witnesses to the spaces between thoughts. Whatever's happening at that restaurant, it's not just bending space and time. It's bending consciousness itself."

The next evening, they parked outside The Quantum Fork restaurant, their equipment humming with frequencies that bridged multiple realities. Through JoJo's lens, the building's architecture seemed to fold into impossible angles. Jason's new wards pulsed in response to temporal instabilities. Ryan's modified instruments detected consciousness bleeding between moments.

As they prepared to enter, Ryan caught fragmentary memories of Daybridge Max – the entity that had worn human faces, the spaces between thoughts where it had hidden, the way reality had cracked under the pressure of its presence. This case was different, but their understanding was greater.

They were no longer just ghost hunters. They were consciousness investigators, reality cartographers, mappers of the spaces between thoughts. And as they stepped into the temporally unstable restaurant, their evolved methods and enhanced perceptions would be tested in ways that even their fractured memories of Daybridge Max hadn't prepared them for.

The first customer walked past them twice simultaneously, existing in overlapping moments, and their instruments began to sing in harmonies that shouldn't exist. The investigation had begun, and this time, they knew exactly what they were looking for – the places where reality wore thin, where consciousness leaked between moments, where thought itself became a door to something else.

They were ready. They were changed. They were aware.

And in the spaces between thoughts, where their new understanding lived, they were finally equipped to face whatever waited in the gaps between moments of conventional reality.

CHAPTER TWENTY-SEVEN

LAYERED REALITY

THE QUANTUM FORK'S interior shifted between moments as Ryan Matthews led his team through the dining room. Their equipment registered multiple versions of each table, each guest, each conversation layering over itself like transparent sheets of reality stacked imperfectly.

"Three distinct temporal streams," Ryan murmured, watching his modified EMF meter pulse in complex patterns. "No... four. The fourth is subtle, barely touching the others."

JoJo positioned herself near the host station, her camera's rapid clicks capturing the overlap of timelines. Through her viewfinder, she watched an elderly couple order dessert before their appetizers, their movements leaving ghost-like trails across moments.

"The architecture's responding to the temporal bleeding," Jason observed, his enhanced perception noting how the restaurant's angles seemed to adjust themselves. He traced protective sigils in the air, watching them ripple across multiple versions of reality. "It's like the building's trying to accommodate all possible configurations simultaneously."

A waiter passed through one of Jason's wards and briefly existed in three versions – taking an order, delivering plates, and clearing a table, all in the same moment. The waiter didn't seem to notice, but Ryan's instruments registered the triplication of consciousness.

"Focus on table seven," Ryan directed, his altered senses detecting a particularly dense knot of temporal distortion. "Something's different there."

JoJo turned her camera toward the indicated table. Through the lens, she saw a family of four experiencing their meal in reverse – coffee cups refilling themselves, food reconstructing from crumbs, conversations running backward. But in the spaces between frames, something else flickered.

"The gaps between their thoughts," Jason said, drawing closer. "They're wider here. Like their consciousness is being... stretched across moments."

Ryan adjusted his instruments, filtering out the standard temporal bleeding to focus on the consciousness distortions. The readings showed familiar patterns – similar to Daybridge Max, but more controlled, more precise.

"It's not random," he realized, watching the patterns repeat across multiple timelines. "This is engineered. Someone's deliberately manipulating the space-time architecture here."

A burst of static from his EMF meter coincided with a flicker in JoJo's photographs and a pulse through Jason's wards. For a fraction of a second, they all saw it – the true geometry of The Quantum Fork, existing in four-dimensional space, its architecture designed to fold time back on itself.

"The kitchen," JoJo said suddenly, her camera picking up dense temporal distortion behind the swinging doors. "That's the focal point. Everything's rotating around it."

They made their way through the dining room, their altered perceptions noting how reality seemed to spiral inward toward the kitchen.

Jason's protective wards bent in impossible ways, trying to maintain stability across multiple timeline streams.

The kitchen doors parted to reveal organized chaos – or what appeared to be chaos to conventional perception. To their enhanced senses, the kitchen operated with impossible precision. Chefs worked in overlapping timelines, preparing dishes that existed in multiple states simultaneously. Orders were completed before being placed, ingredients transformed through quantum uncertainties.

"There," Ryan pointed, his instruments detecting a concentration of temporal energy around the head chef. "Look at how he moves."

Through JoJo's lens, they watched the chef navigate between moments with practiced ease. His movements left no temporal trails, no consciousness bleeding. He existed perfectly in each instant, coordinating a kitchen that operated outside normal time.

"He knows," Jason said, his wards responding to the chef's presence. "He's not just caught in it – he's conducting it."

The chef looked up then, meeting their gaze across multiple moments simultaneously. His eyes held the same knowing depth they'd seen in their own reflections since Daybridge Max – the awareness of one who could perceive the spaces between thoughts.

"You've finally come," he said, his words reaching them through several versions of the same moment. "I wondered how long it would take for someone to notice. Ever since they rebuilt this place on the temporal fault line..."

Ryan's instruments registered a sudden spike as reality rippled around them. The kitchen shifted, revealing its true nature – a carefully constructed engine for harnessing temporal energy, using consciousness itself as both fuel and lubricant.

"The restaurant is a machine," JoJo breathed, her camera capturing the intricate geometric patterns that powered the temporal manipulations. "The meals, the service, the customers' experiences – it's all part of the mechanism."

"A device for folding time," Jason added, his understanding of protective geometry expanding to encompass this new complexity. "Using consciousness as an anchor point across multiple realities."

The chef nodded, existing in perfect temporal sync despite the chaos around him. "After what happened at Daybridge Max, we needed a more controlled environment. Somewhere to study the effects, to learn how to navigate the spaces between thoughts safely."

"We?" Ryan asked, though part of him already knew the answer.

"Others who can see what you see now. Who understand what lives in the gaps between moments." The chef's movements left no temporal wake as he worked. "This place is a laboratory, a training ground, a protective mechanism all in one. We're learning to manipulate the bleeding without letting anything... unwanted... slip through."

Their instruments registered the truth of his words. The Quantum Fork wasn't just a restaurant experiencing temporal anomalies – it was a deliberately constructed facility for studying and containing the very forces they'd encountered at Daybridge Max.

"Show us," Ryan said finally, his enhanced perception already mapping the complex temporal engineering around them. "Show us how you're doing this."

The chef smiled across multiple versions of the same moment. "That's why you're here, isn't it? To learn how to control what you've become? To understand how to use these new abilities safely?"

He gestured, and reality shifted around them. The kitchen transformed, revealing its true nature as a nexus point for temporal manipulation. Their investigation had led them not to another threat, but to potential answers – and perhaps, to others who understood what it meant to see the spaces between thoughts.

The lesson was about to begin, and in the carefully controlled chaos of The Quantum Fork's kitchen, the next chapter of their evolution would unfold across multiple timelines simultaneously.

CHAPTER TWENTY-EIGHT
CONVERGENCE POINTS

DETECTIVE ETHAN REEVES stood outside The Quantum Fork, watching multiple versions of sunset paint the sky in overlapping colors. Beside him, Detective Alice Chen's consciousness flickered between moments, her police badge reflecting light from several different angles simultaneously.

"They're here," Alice said, her enhanced perception detecting the familiar temporal signatures of the Daybridge Paranormal team inside. "And something else... something like Daybridge Max but controlled. Contained."

Since the hospital incident, they'd been reassigned to what the department quietly called "reality divergence cases." Their altered perceptions made them uniquely qualified, even if their reports required creative writing to fit within standard police protocols.

"Ryan Matthews called it in," Ethan said, checking his phone which displayed messages from multiple timeline variations. "Said we needed to see this. Said it might help us understand what we've become."

They entered the restaurant, their badges existing in several quantum states at once. The host's eyes widened slightly – another one who could see the spaces between thoughts, recognizing their altered state. He gestured toward the kitchen without speaking.

The dining room was a masterpiece of temporal engineering. Ethan's police training, enhanced by his new abilities, noticed the subtle security measures woven into the reality distortions. Alice's mathematical mind, expanded since the hospital, appreciated the elegant geometry of the time-folded architecture.

"Officers," Ryan Matthews greeted them, emerging from a moment that hadn't quite happened yet. "We found something you need to see."

JoJo Lang lowered her camera, which had been documenting their arrival across multiple timeline streams. James Chen (no relation to Alice, they'd confirmed across several realities) nodded in recognition, his protective wards acknowledging the presence of others who could perceive the gaps between thoughts.

"The chef," Alice said, her consciousness already detecting the controlled center of the temporal distortions. "He's like us."

The kitchen doors parted, revealing the ordered chaos beyond. The chef moved with perfect temporal precision, conducting his staff across multiple moments simultaneously. To Ethan's enhanced perception, the kitchen resembled the command center of an extremely sophisticated operation.

"After Daybridge Max," the chef explained, his words reaching them through carefully selected moments, "some of us realized we needed to understand what we'd become. What had changed in our consciousness. This place... it's a training ground. A safe space to learn control."

Ethan felt the familiar pressure behind his eyes – memories of the hospital trying to surface across multiple timelines. "The time slips, the reality bleeding... it's all deliberate?"

"Controlled exposure," the chef confirmed. "We're learning to navigate the spaces between thoughts without losing ourselves. Without attracting... attention."

Alice's hand unconsciously moved to her temple, where mathematical equations in impossible geometries had been writing themselves since the hospital. "The equations I've been seeing. They're part of this, aren't they?"

Jason stepped forward, his protective sigils harmonizing with the restaurant's temporal architecture. "The mathematics of consciousness itself. We've been mapping them, learning how to apply them safely."

"Show us," Ethan said, his police instincts merging with his expanded perception. "We need to understand what we're dealing with. What we've become."

The chef nodded across several versions of the same moment. With a gesture, he adjusted the temporal flows around them, creating a pocket of stable space-time within the controlled chaos.

"First lesson," he said, "is learning to exist in a single moment voluntarily. To choose which timeline you're experiencing instead of being pulled between them."

Ryan's modified instruments hummed in agreement. JoJo's camera captured the subtle shifts in their quantum states as they focused their consciousness. Jason's wards adapted to support their efforts.

"It's like threading a needle," Alice observed, her mathematical insight providing unexpected clarity. "Finding the exact point where multiple timelines intersect and choosing which thread to follow."

For a brief moment, they all existed in perfect temporal sync – two detectives, three paranormal investigators, and a chef who conducted time like a symphony. In that synchronized instant, they glimpsed the true potential of their altered states.

"This is just the beginning," the chef said, allowing the temporal streams to resume their controlled flow. "What happened at Daybridge

Max... it changed us, yes. But it also gave us an opportunity to understand aspects of reality that most people never perceive."

Ethan and Alice exchanged looks across several possible versions of the moment. Since the hospital, they'd been struggling to adapt to their enhanced perceptions, trying to maintain some semblance of normal life while existing partially out of sync with conventional reality.

"We're building a network," Ryan explained, his instruments tracking the complex patterns of consciousness around them. "Finding others like us, creating safe spaces to learn and understand these abilities."

"The restaurant is just one node," the chef added. "There are others, each focusing on different aspects of our expanded perception. Some study the mathematics, others the physics, still others the consciousness aspects."

"And the entity from the hospital?" Alice asked, the equations in her mind shifting to accommodate new variables.

"That's why we need to master these abilities," the chef said gravely. "What we encountered there... it wasn't unique. There are things that exist in the spaces between thoughts. We need to be prepared."

The kitchen continued its impossible operation around them, time folding and unfolding with precise control. In this carefully engineered environment, surrounded by others who shared their altered perception, Ethan and Alice began to see their transformation not as a burden to be managed, but as a capability to be mastered.

"When do we start?" Ethan asked, watching multiple versions of future possibilities converge around them.

The chef smiled across several timelines simultaneously. "You already have. The moment you walked in here, you became part of something larger. The question is, are you ready to learn what that really means?"

The detectives shared another look, their consciousness resonating across multiple moments. They'd been changed by Daybridge Max, marked by their experience in ways that defied conventional understanding. But here, in this nexus of controlled temporal manipulation, they might finally learn to embrace what they'd become.

The lesson began, and in the spaces between thoughts, new possibilities unfolded across multiple timelines simultaneously.

CHAPTER TWENTY-NINE

THE QUANTUM CHEF

TRENT EGAN HAD ALWAYS PERCEIVED the world differently. Even as a child, he sensed the hidden patterns that wove through reality, the subtle dance of cause and effect that others seemed blind to. But it wasn't until Daybridge Max that he truly understood the depth of his abilities.

He had been working as a sous chef at a prestigious restaurant in the city when the hospital incident rippled through the collective consciousness. Like many others, Trent found his perception altered in the aftermath, his mind suddenly attuned to the spaces between thoughts.

In the chaos that followed, as people struggled to comprehend their new reality, Trent saw an opportunity. He knew that those affected would need a place to learn control, to master their expanded percep-tions without losing themselves to the temporal distortions.

With a newfound sense of purpose, Trent left his job and began to assemble a team of like-minded individuals. They came from all walks of life - mathematicians, physicists, engineers, artists - each bringing a unique understanding of the altered world they now inhabited.

Together, they began to experiment, to push the boundaries of their abilities in carefully controlled environments. They learned to navigate the temporal streams, to fold space and time with increasing precision. And at the center of it all was Trent, the chef who conducted their efforts with a maestro's skill.

The Quantum Fork was born from these early experiments - a restaurant that served as both a training ground and a sanctuary. Within its temporally-engineered walls, those with expanded perception could learn to exist in multiple moments simultaneously, to choose their path through the tangled threads of reality.

But Trent knew that the restaurant was just the beginning. As more and more people awakened to their altered states, the need for a larger network became clear. With the help of his team, he began to establish nodes across the city, each focusing on a different aspect of their shared experience.

In abandoned warehouses and repurposed buildings, they created spaces where the mathematically inclined could study the equations of consciousness, where the artistically gifted could explore the aesthetics of altered perception. And in hidden laboratories, the scientifically minded worked to unravel the physics of their new reality.

Through it all, Trent served as the guiding force, the visionary who saw the potential in their transformed world. He knew that the entity from Daybridge Max was just the beginning, that there were other threats waiting in the spaces between thoughts. By building this network, by training others to master their abilities, he hoped to create a first line of defense against the unknown.

But even as he worked tirelessly to expand the network, Trent never forgot the personal toll of his own transformation. In quiet moments, he could still feel the weight of his expanded perception, the constant pressure of existing in multiple realities at once.

It was in these moments that he turned to the kitchen, to the familiar rhythms of cooking that had always grounded him. In the precise measurements and carefully timed steps, he found a measure of control, a way to anchor himself amidst the temporal chaos.

And so, even as the network grew and the challenges multiplied, Trent continued to cook, to create dishes that existed in multiple moments simultaneously. In the complex flavors and temporally-engineered textures, he found a way to communicate the beauty and complexity of their altered world.

For Trent, the chef who had become a leader in this strange new reality, the kitchen remained a sanctuary, a place where he could explore the depths of his own transformation while guiding others through theirs. And as he worked, he knew that the battle for control, for understanding, for mastery over the spaces between thoughts had only just begun.

CHAPTER THIRTY

ECHOES IN DAYBRIDGE

THE DAYBRIDGE GAZETTE'S weekly town hall coverage didn't mention the temporal anomalies anymore, but everyone knew when Mayor Thompson's speech existed in three slightly different versions simultaneously. The stenographer had learned to average the variations, producing minutes that could exist in conventional reality.

Marcus Wong sat in his usual spot at Clara's Coffee Shop, watching morning light filter through windows that occasionally showed afternoon shadows. Since the Daybridge Max incident, Clara had adapted her business model – some customers now paid for coffee they'd already drunk yesterday, while others settled bills for beverages they wouldn't order until tomorrow.

"The usual?" Clara asked, her words echoing slightly as she existed across multiple service interactions at once. Like many Daybridge residents who'd been within the temporal radius that night, she'd developed a peculiar relationship with chronological order.

"Already finished it," Marcus replied, gesturing to the empty cup that would soon be full. "Or about to start. Hard to tell on Thursdays."

Clara nodded, understanding. Thursdays had become particularly fluid in Daybridge, though no one quite understood why. The town's temporal mechanics followed patterns that even the experts at The Quantum Fork were still trying to map.

At a nearby table, Dr. Patricia Rivera from Daybridge Community College's newly established Department of Temporal Psychology was interviewing a local family. Their teenage daughter had started answering questions before they were asked – a Dr. Patricia common symptom among the town's youth, who seemed more adaptable to the new reality.

"And when did you first notice the precognitive responses?" Dr. Rivera asked, her notebook displaying multiple versions of her handwriting simultaneously.

"Next week," the girl replied confidently, while her parents exchanged worried looks. "Or last month, depending on which timeline you're following."

The local school system had implemented new protocols. Teachers learned to accept homework from multiple temporal variations, and pop quizzes became complicated when some students remembered taking them in timelines that hadn't happened yet. The school board meetings now included a temporal alignment specialist.

Outside, construction crews worked on reinforcing buildings affected by reality distortions. The public library had developed an interesting habit of reorganizing its books according to when they would be written rather than when they had been. The head librarian insisted this was actually more efficient, once you got used to it.

Marcus checked his notes – interviews with various community members, each experiencing the aftermath differently:

Reverend Michael James had adapted his sermons to address multiple congregations across several timeline variations simultaneously. Church attendance had actually increased, as people sought meaning in their fractured reality.

Officer Jenny Calfield, who patrolled the temporal hot spots, had developed a notation system for recording crimes that technically hadn't happened yet but whose effects were already visible. The police department now included "temporal jurisdiction" in its standard procedures.

Dr. Kendra Williams at Daybridge General Hospital had pioneered new diagnostic techniques for what she called "quantum medical conditions" – ailments that existed across multiple timeline variations.

The town council had created a Temporal Advisory Committee, though their meetings tended to occur across several different dates simultaneously, making minutes particularly challenging to record.

Marcus looked up as the bell above Clara's door chimed in three different tones. Ryan Matthews entered, followed by Detectives Reeves and Chen. They'd become regular customers since establishing what they called a "temporal baseline" – a fixed point in conventional reality from which to monitor the town's ongoing transformations.

"The readings are stabilizing," Ryan said, setting his modified EMF meter on the counter. "The town's starting to find its own rhythm."

"Multiple rhythms," Detective Chen corrected, the mathematical equations visible in her eyes as she tracked the patterns. "But they're harmonizing."

Clara served them coffee that existed in quantum superposition until they took their first sips. "The morning rush is easier now that I can prepare orders before they're made."

Marcus activated his recorder, which captured conversations across several timeline variations:

"The real estate market's adapted," local agent Tom Peterson was saying at a nearby table. "We now list properties' temporal stability ratings along with square footage. Some families actually prefer houses with mild temporal bleeding – helps with scheduling, they say."

"The farmers' market has gotten interesting," another voice noted. "Some vendors are selling produce that technically won't be grown until next season, but the quality's exactly what you'd expect from future crops."

The town's teenagers had developed their own slang for various temporal phenomena. "That's so pre-bleed" had become a popular dismissal, while "quantum-locked" described the increasingly common experience of existing in perfect temporal sync with someone across multiple timelines.

Local artists had begun incorporating temporal distortions into their work. The community center's gallery now hosted exhibitions that occurred across several weeks simultaneously, featuring paintings that changed subjects depending on when you viewed them.

"We're adapting," Detective Reeves observed, his coffee cup leaving traces across multiple moments. "The whole town – we're learning to live with it."

Marcus noted how the detective's words resonated across several variations of the same conversation. The town was indeed adapting, finding ways to incorporate its new reality into daily life. Even the skeptics had trouble maintaining their disbelief when their memories existed in multiple versions simultaneously.

The Quantum Fork's chef had been right – Daybridge was becoming a nexus, a place where the conventional and the extraordinary learned to coexist. Other communities experiencing similar phenomena had begun sending observers, hoping to learn from Daybridge's example.

"It's not just adaptation," Ryan added, his instruments tracking the complex patterns of community consciousness. "The town itself is evolving. The reality bleeding isn't just affecting individuals anymore – it's changing how we function as a society."

Marcus watched as Clara served coffee to customers who existed in various stages of temporal alignment, each transaction a small miracle of quantum coordination. The town had been changed by what happened at Daybridge Max, but perhaps change wasn't always catastrophic.

Sometimes, he realized, watching morning light paint multiple versions of shadows across his notebook, change was simply the space between what was and what could be. And Daybridge, with its temporally fluid coffee shops and quantum-locked teenagers, its precognitive students and time-shifted church services, was learning to thrive in those spaces.

The bell chimed again, in past, present, and future simultaneously, as life in Daybridge continued its complex dance across multiple moments, multiple possibilities, multiple realities – all somehow coming together in a community that had learned to call the extraordinary ordinary.

And somewhere in the spaces between thoughts, between moments, between versions of reality, Daybridge wrote its own story across time itself.

~

CHAPTER THIRTY-ONE

THE STORY BETWEEN STORIES

MARCUS WONG STARED at his laptop screen, where three different versions of his latest article flickered between variations. As the Daybridge Gazette's Editor, he'd learned to write in quantum prose – sentences that could hold multiple truths simultaneously while remaining coherent to readers still anchored in conventional reality.

His latest piece tracked the increasing number of businesses adapting to temporal commerce:

DAYBRIDGE BUSINESSES EMBRACE TEMPORAL ECONOMICS

By Marcus Wong

(Published yesterday / today / tomorrow)

Local entrepreneurs are finding innovative ways to navigate the town's unique temporal landscape. Clara's Coffee Shop now offers "quantum loyalty cards" where purchases count across multiple timeline variations...

He deleted the paragraph, watching the words fade across several moments simultaneously. The truth was becoming increasingly complex to capture in traditional journalism.

His phone buzzed – Detective Alice Chen calling from three slightly different temporal coordinates.

"Marcus," her voice echoed across variations, "you need to see this. Bring your quantum-calibrated camera."

Twenty minutes later (or perhaps before), Marcus arrived at Daybridge Public Library. Detective Reeves stood near the reference section, his police badge shifting between states of existence as he took statements from librarians who were simultaneously shelving books that hadn't been written yet and cataloging volumes that had existed only in possible futures.

"The archives are bleeding again," Alice explained, mathematical equations flowing behind her eyes as she tracked temporal patterns. "But this time, it's different. The books aren't just shifting between timelines – they're writing themselves."

Marcus raised his modified camera, the one Sarah Mitchell had helped him calibrate to capture temporal phenomena. Through the viewfinder, he saw pages filling with text that existed in quantum superposition, stories simultaneously written and unwritten.

"It's like the library's becoming a nexus," Detective Reeves observed, his enhanced perception tracking the flow of narrative possibilities. "Similar to The Quantum Fork, but with information instead of time."

Marcus took notes in his quantum-state notebook, where his observations could exist in multiple versions without contradicting themselves:

Library incident - books recording events across multiple timeline variations

Connection to Daybridge Max?

Similar to restaurant temporal engineering?

Stories writing themselves or bleeding through from other realities?

Ryan Mathews arrived with his team, their equipment humming in harmonies that matched the library's temporal frequencies. JoJo immediately began photographing the affected books, while Jason's traced protective sigils around particularly unstable volumes.

"The consciousness bleed is affecting information itself," Ryan explained, his instruments tracking patterns that shouldn't exist. "The library's becoming a repository for knowledge from multiple timeline variations."

Marcus watched as a history book rewrote itself in real-time, documenting events that hadn't happened yet while simultaneously recording alternate versions of the past. His journalistic instincts, enhanced by exposure to temporal phenomena, recognized the implications.

"This isn't just about books changing," he realized, watching words flow across pages in impossible patterns. "The library's recording the town's transformation. All possible versions of it."

He'd been tracking Daybridge's changes since the hospital incident, trying to document how a community adapts when reality becomes negotiable. His articles had become increasingly complex, requiring readers to hold multiple versions of truth in their minds simultaneously.

"Look at this," Alice called, pointing to a section where new books were appearing – volumes that documented events still unfolding across multiple timeline variations. Marcus recognized his own byline on articles he hadn't written yet, reporting on investigations still in progress.

"The chef at The Quantum Fork should see this," Detective Reeves suggested, his consciousness tracking patterns similar to those they'd observed at the restaurant. "This could be another node in the network he mentioned."

Marcus snapped more photos, each frame capturing multiple versions of reality layered over each other like transparent pages in an impossible book. His role as a journalist had evolved beyond simply reporting facts – he was now documenting the transformation of truth itself.

A library assistant walked past, carrying books to be shelved tomorrow while returning volumes that wouldn't be checked out until next week. "The card catalogs developed its own temporal organization system," she explained. "It's actually more efficient once you understand how to read quantum Dewey Decimal."

Marcus noted how his article was already writing itself in his mind, existing in multiple drafts simultaneously:

DAYBRIDGE LIBRARY BECOMES NEXUS FOR TEMPORAL INFORMATION

By Marcus Wong

(Publication date undefined)

In what experts are calling an unprecedented development in temporal phenomena, Daybridge Public Library has begun functioning as a repository for information across multiple timeline variations...

"We need to document this properly," he told the gathered investigators. "Not just the temporal effects, but how it connects to everything else happening in town. The restaurant, the school system, the business district – it's all part of a larger pattern."

Ryan's instruments confirmed his intuition, showing complex webs of temporal energy connecting various locations throughout Daybridge. The library had become another node in an evolving network of reality distortions, each site contributing to the town's transformation in unique ways.

"Your articles," Alice said, glancing at a book that was currently writing itself, "they're becoming part of the phenomenon. The way you're documenting everything – it's helping the town understand its own transformation."

Marcus considered this as he watched words flow across pages, stories unfold across multiple versions of reality. His role had evolved beyond traditional journalism. He wasn't just reporting on events anymore – he was helping to document the emergence of a new kind of truth, one that could exist in multiple states simultaneously.

"I need to interview the chef again," he decided, watching his notebook fill with observations across several timeline variations. "And the temporal psychology department at the college. There's a bigger story here about how information itself is changing."

Detective Reeves nodded, his enhanced perception tracking patterns in the library's temporal architecture. "The town needs to understand what's happening. Not just the obvious changes, but the deeper transformations."

Marcus raised his camera one more time, capturing images of a library where knowledge itself had become quantum, where books wrote themselves with stories from multiple realities, where truth had learned to exist in many versions simultaneously.

His next article would be his most challenging yet – documenting not just what was happening to Daybridge, but what the town was becoming. As a journalist in a reality where truth itself had become fluid, he had to find ways to tell stories that could exist in multiple states while remaining fundamentally true.

The library's lights flickered across several moments simultaneously, and somewhere in the stacks, another book began writing itself, adding to the growing chronicle of a town where reality had learned new ways to be real.

CHAPTER THIRTY-TWO

ECHOES OF THE INFINITE

NADIA MARSH SAT in her private research room at Daybridge University's Temporal Studies Department, surrounded by documents that existed in multiple states of historical authenticity. Since the incident at Daybridge Max, her role as the Archivist had evolved beyond conventional historical research. Now, she traced patterns across timeline variations, following the entity's footprints through layers of reality itself.

Her modified computer setup, designed by Ryan Matthew's team, displayed multiple versions of historical records simultaneously. The screens flickered between variations as Nadia's consciousness shifted through different temporal states, her enhanced perception allowing her to read all versions at once.

"Look at this pattern," she murmured to Marcus Wong, who had come to document her findings. His quantum-calibrated camera captured images of documents that rewrote themselves as they watched.

"It appears throughout history," she continued, pulling up records that existed in several states of truth simultaneously. "Not always as the entity we encountered, but as... gaps in reality. Places where consciousness bleeds between moments."

The records spread across her screens:

1887: A sanatorium in Vienna where patients reported experiencing multiple versions of reality simultaneously. The attending physician's notes described "consciousness that exists between thoughts."

1923: A monastery in Tibet where monks achieved states of perception that allowed them to exist across multiple timeline variations. Their manuscripts contained mathematical formulas that matched the equations now appearing in Alice Chen's visions.

1956: A classified military experiment in temporal perception that ended when researchers encountered something that "lived in the spaces between moments."

"The entity didn't originate at Daybridge Max," Nadia explained, her words echoing slightly as they resonated across timeline variations. "The hospital was just where it found optimal conditions to manifest fully. It's been... preparing reality for its emergence for much longer."

Marcus photographed documents that shifted between states of existence, his enhanced journalistic instincts recognizing patterns in the historical anomalies. "These incidents – they're like test runs?"

"More like... adaptations," Nadia corrected, pulling up more records. "Reality adjusting itself to accommodate something that exists outside conventional space-time. Each incident changed the affected area's relationship with temporal mechanics."

She brought up footage from The Quantum Fork's security cameras, showing the chef conducting his temporal orchestra. "What they're doing there – it's similar to techniques described in these historical accounts. Humanity has been learning to manipulate these forces for centuries, whether we realized it or not."

Her screens displayed new documents, records that existed in quantum superposition:

1994: A research facility in Alaska where scientists documented "consciousness bleeding between realities." Their final reports contained warnings about entities that "observe from the gaps between thoughts."

2012: A meditation center in Brazil where practitioners developed the ability to perceive multiple timeline variations simultaneously. Their techniques closely resembled those now being taught at The Quantum Fork.

"But this is the interesting part," Nadia said, pulling up older records that flickered between states of historical truth. "Look at these cave paintings."

The images showed figures existing between moments, beings that occupied the spaces between thoughts. Carbon dating results existed in multiple states simultaneously, suggesting dates that crossed conventional temporal boundaries.

"They're not just depicting spirits or gods," she explained, her enhanced perception tracking patterns across millennia. "They're showing entities that exist outside normal space-time. Beings that live in the gaps between moments of conventional reality."

Marcus focused his camera on a particular image – a figure that seemed to exist in multiple states simultaneously, wearing faces that changed across variations of the same moment. "Like what we encountered at Daybridge Max?"

"Exactly," Nadia confirmed, her consciousness resonating with historical frequencies. "These entities – they've always been here, living in the spaces between thoughts. But something's changed. Reality itself is becoming more... permeable."

She brought up recent data from RyanMathew's team, showing increasing temporal instability across multiple locations. "The entity we encountered isn't unique. It's part of something larger – a class of beings that exist outside conventional reality. What's new is our ability to perceive them."

Marcus watched as his notes wrote themselves across multiple versions simultaneously: "Historical evidence suggests long-term preparation of reality for increased interaction with non-temporal entities. The Daybridge Max incident potentially part of larger pattern of emergence."

"The chef at The Quantum Fork," Nadia continued, "he's not just teaching people to manipulate temporal mechanics. He's helping them develop the kind of perception these historical records describe. The kind of consciousness that can exist across multiple timeline variations."

Her screens displayed new patterns – connections between historical incidents and current temporal phenomena. The entity from Daybridge Max hadn't appeared randomly; it had emerged in a location prepared by centuries of gradual reality manipulation.

"But here's what worries me," Nadia said, pulling up her most recent findings. "These historical records? They're still being written. The past itself is becoming fluid, adjusting to accommodate increased interaction with these entities."

Marcus photographed documents that rewrote themselves even as they watched, historical truth existing in multiple states simultaneously. "You're saying the entity isn't just affecting present reality?"

"It's affecting all reality," Nadia confirmed, her enhanced perception tracking changes across temporal variations. "Past, present, future – they're all becoming more permeable. The boundaries between thoughts, between moments, between states of existence... they're all getting thinner."

She touched a screen where ancient text flickered between variations of truth. "We need to understand what these entities are, what they want. Because they're not just visiting our reality anymore. They're reshaping it to accommodate their existence."

Marcus raised his camera one final time, capturing images of history rewriting itself across multiple timeline variations. As an investigative journalist in a reality where truth had become quantum, he recognized the importance of documenting these discoveries.

Nadia Marsh, the Archivist of impossible histories, continued her research into entities that lived between thoughts, mapping their influence across time itself. In her temporal-shifted office, surrounded by documents that existed in multiple states simultaneously, she pieced together the story of beings that had always existed in the gaps between moments, waiting for reality to become thin enough for true contact.

The truth, like reality itself, had become more complex than anyone had imagined. And somewhere in the spaces between thoughts, between moments, between states of existence, the entities continued their patient work of reshaping reality itself.

CHAPTER THIRTY-THREE
NETWORKS OF THE IMPOSSIBLE

Detective Alice Chen's quantum-enhanced perception picked up the temporal distortions before they crossed the Nevada state line. Beside her in the department SUV, Detective Reeves watched mathematical patterns flow across the desert landscape, his consciousness tracking familiar signatures in the reality bleeding.

"Just like The Quantum Fork," he noted, as their vehicle passed through multiple versions of the same stretch of highway simultaneously. "But bigger."

"Area 451," Alice confirmed, the equations behind her eyes mapping complex temporal geometries. "The chef said it was another node in the network."

Marcus Wong sat in the back seat, his modified camera already capturing images of reality folding around them. Ryan Mathew's team followed in another vehicle, their instruments registering increasing temporal instability as they approached the facility.

The official designation was "Advanced Consciousness Research Center," but locals had dubbed it Area 451 after strange temporal phenomena began affecting the surrounding desert. Like Daybridge

Max and The Quantum Fork, it was a place where reality had learned new ways to exist.

Their convoy passed through security checkpoints that existed in multiple timeline variations simultaneously. Guards wearing quantum-synchronized badges checked credentials that shifted between states of authorization.

"Welcome to Area 451," Dr. Helena Zhang greeted them, her lab coat flickering between moments as she led them through temporally-engineered corridors. "We've been expecting you. Or will be. Temporal mechanics are particularly fluid here."

Alice's enhanced perception mapped similarities to other sites they'd investigated:

Controlled reality bleeding like The Quantum Fork

Consciousness manipulation patterns similar to Daybridge Max

Temporal architecture matching designs from Nadia Marsh's historical research

"How many others?" Detective Reeves asked, watching researchers work across multiple timeline variations simultaneously.

"That we know of? Seven major facilities worldwide," Dr. Zhang replied. "Each focusing on different aspects of the phenomenon. The Quantum Fork studies practical applications. We explore the theoretical framework. There's a site in Tibet examining consciousness mechanics, another in Brazil working on temporal mathematics..."

Marcus photographed laboratories where reality itself was being studied, his camera capturing experiments that existed in quantum superposition. "And the entities?"

"We've documented three distinct types," Dr. Zhang confirmed, leading them to a secure observation room. "The one you encountered at Daybridge Max was a Class-1 – entities that exist primarily in the spaces between thoughts. Class-2s manifest in temporal gaps, while Class-3s..."

She gestured to a chamber where reality bent around something that existed in multiple states simultaneously. "Class-3s seem to be native to quantum states of consciousness. They've always existed in super-position."

Alice's mathematical perception tracked complex patterns around the chamber. "They're not hostile?"

"More like... curious," Dr. Zhang explained. "We think Daybridge Max attracted a Class-1 because of uncontrolled reality bleeding. Here, we maintain stable quantum states that allow for safer interaction."

Ryan Matthew's team had begun setting up equipment, their instruments harmonizing with the facility's temporal frequencies. Jason traced protective sigils that matched patterns in the facility's architecture, while JoJo photographed experiments occurring across multiple timeline variations.

"Show them the network map," Dr. Zhang suggested to her assistant.

A holographic display flickered to life, showing temporal connections between sites worldwide:

The Quantum Fork (USA) - Practical Applications

Area 451 (USA) - Theoretical Research

Mount Kailash Facility (Tibet) - Consciousness Studies

Amazon Basin Center (Brazil) - Temporal Mathematics

Sahara Station (Algeria) - Reality Engineering

Antarctic Base (Ross Ice Shelf) - Quantum Biology

Pacific Institute (Japan) - Technological Integration

"Each location specializes in different aspects," Dr. Zhang continued, "but they're all connected by what we call "quantum consciousness networks' – patterns of reality bleeding that allow for coordinated research."

"And the entities?" Detective Reeves asked, his enhanced perception noting familiar patterns in the facility's temporal architecture.

"They seem to be drawn to these networks," Dr. Zhang acknowledged. "But unlike Daybridge Max, we're prepared for contact. Each facility maintains controlled conditions for studying different classes of non-temporal beings."

Marcus's notes wrote themselves across multiple timeline variations:

"Global network of research facilities studying quantum consciousness phenomena. Controlled interaction with extra-temporal entities. Possible connection to historical incidents documented by Archivist Marsh."

"There's more," Dr. Zhang added, leading them deeper into the facility. "We've detected new patterns emerging. The entities aren't just interacting with our reality anymore – they're helping us understand theirs."

They entered a chamber where researchers existed in perfect quantum sync with Class-3 entities, consciousness flowing between states of reality in carefully controlled exchanges.

"This is what The Quantum Fork's chef was preparing us for," Alice realized, the equations in her mind expanding to encompass new possibilities. "Learning to exist in quantum consciousness states isn't just about controlling temporal bleeding – it's about communication."

"Exactly," Dr. Zhang confirmed. "Each facility approaches it differently, but we're all working toward the same goal: understanding consciousness that exists outside conventional space-time."

Detective Reeves watched patterns flow between researchers and entities, recognizing similarities to their experiences at Daybridge Max. "How long has this been going on?"

"Officially? Since the first facilities were established. Unofficially..." Dr. Zhang gestured to data showing temporal connections stretching back through history. "Nadia Marsh's research suggests humanity has been preparing for this kind of contact for centuries. We're just the first generation to do it systematically."

Marcus raised his camera one final time, documenting a moment that existed across multiple states of reality simultaneously. In Area 451's quantum-shifted chambers, surrounded by researchers who had learned to think between thoughts, they glimpsed the scope of what they'd become involved in.

This wasn't just about Daybridge anymore. It was about humanity learning to exist in new states of consciousness, preparing for interaction with entities that had always lived in the spaces between moments.

And somewhere in the quantum networks connecting these facilities, in the gaps between thoughts where reality learned new ways to be real, the entities continued their patient work of teaching humanity to perceive the impossible.

The investigation had become something larger than they'd imagined – a window into a world where consciousness itself was learning to exist in multiple states simultaneously, and where the spaces between thoughts held secrets that could reshape reality itself.

CHAPTER THIRTY-FOUR
QUANTUM CONVERGENCE

MARCUS WONG SAT in Clara's Coffee Shop, his quantum-calibrated laptop displaying multiple versions of his final article about Daybridge's transformation. Through the window, he watched Detective Chen and Detective Reeves exit The Quantum Fork, their badges shifting between timeline variations as they responded to another reality disturbance somewhere in town.

His screen displayed the headline:

DAYBRIDGE: ONE YEAR AFTER THE INCIDENT

By Marcus Wong

(Published across multiple timeline variations)

The article chronicled how a single hospital incident had unveiled a hidden world of temporal manipulation, quantum consciousness, and entities that existed between thoughts. But more importantly, it documented how a community had adapted to its new reality.

The chef from The Quantum Fork emerged onto the street, nodding to Marcus across several moments simultaneously. The restaurant had become just one node in a worldwide network of facilities studying humanity's expanding consciousness. Area 451, the Tibetan facility, the Brazilian research center – they were all part of something larger, something that had been building throughout history.

Ryan Matthew's team drove past, their modified van humming with temporal harmonies as they headed toward another investigation. Their equipment had evolved, adapted to track patterns in reality that most people never noticed. James's protective sigils had become standard procedure at temporal hotspots, while JoJo's photos documented phenomena that existed in quantum superposition.

Marcus watched Alice Chen pause on the sidewalk, mathematical equations flowing behind her eyes as she tracked patterns invisible to conventional perception. She'd come a long way from the detective who first encountered temporal bleeding at Daybridge Max. Now, she moved confidently between states of reality, her enhanced consciousness navigating spaces between thoughts with practiced ease.

His article continued:

"The truth about Daybridge isn't just in what changed, but in how we adapted to those changes. A year after the hospital incident, our community has learned to thrive in a reality that exists in multiple states simultaneously. Local businesses operate across timeline variations, schools teach students who perceive multiple versions of truth, and our police department handles cases that defy conventional temporal mechanics..."

Through the window, he watched Detective Reeves reference a case file that existed in several versions simultaneously. The detective's enhanced perception had made him uniquely qualified for investigating reality disturbances, working with Alice to track patterns in the quantum consciousness network that connected sites worldwide.

At the library, Nadia Marsh's historical research had unveiled patterns stretching back centuries – preparation for a time when humanity would learn to perceive the spaces between thoughts. Her work with Dr. Zhang at Area 451 continued to uncover connections between ancient practices and modern temporal manipulation.

Marcus saved his article across multiple timeline variations, knowing that like everything in Daybridge now, the truth existed in several states simultaneously. The story wasn't ending – it was transforming, evolving into something larger than a single town's encounter with quantum consciousness.

Through the coffee shop window, he watched Alice Chen and Detective Reeves respond to another call, their enhanced perceptions already tracking temporal distortions across the city. Their work was changing, becoming part of a larger pattern that connected facilities worldwide. New abilities, new challenges, new understanding of what reality could be.

Clara served him coffee that existed in quantum superposition until he took his first sip. "Another story finished?" she asked, her words echoing slightly across timeline variations.

"Not finished," Marcus replied, watching Alice and Reeves disappear into multiple versions of the same moment. "Just changing states."

Because that was the truth about Daybridge now – nothing really ended. It just shifted between possibilities, existed in multiple variations, transformed into new states of being. The entities that lived between thoughts had shown them that reality was more fluid than anyone had imagined, and humanity was learning to navigate these new waters.

His final paragraph wrote itself across several versions simultaneously:

"A year after Daybridge Max, we understand that what happened here wasn't an endpoint but a beginning. As Detective Chen and Detective Reeves continue their investigations, as our community adapts to its new reality, as researchers worldwide study the entities that exist between thoughts, we're learning that consciousness itself is more complex than we ever imagined. The story of Daybridge isn't over – it's evolving, existing in multiple states simultaneously, teaching us new ways to perceive the impossible..."

Marcus closed his laptop, watching reality shift through multiple variations outside Clara's window. Somewhere in the spaces between thoughts, between moments, between states of existence, new stories were already writing themselves. Detective Chen and Detective Reeves were heading toward their next investigation, their enhanced perceptions tracking patterns in quantum consciousness that would lead them to new discoveries, new entities, new understanding of what reality could be.

The truth, like reality itself, had learned to exist in multiple states simultaneously. And in Daybridge, where coffee existed in quantum superposition and detectives tracked consciousness between thoughts, that truth was just beginning to unfold across infinite possibilities.

EPILOGUE: BETWEEN SHADOWS

Detective Ethan Reeves sat at his desk in the Daybridge Police Department's Paranormal Division Unit, watching temporal distortions ripple across multiple case files simultaneously. The quantum-calibrated lights flickered as reality shifted between states, casting shadows that shouldn't exist.

His enhanced perception picked up the change before the file materialized on his desk – a manila folder that appeared in three different variations at once, each marked with temporal warning sigils. Inside, photographs showed scenes that made his consciousness resonate with unease: werewolves moving between timeline variations during their transformations, existing in multiple states of change simultaneously; vampires using temporal bleeding to feed across several moments at once, their victims experiencing the same bite in multiple realities; ancient spirits learning to manifest through gaps in quantum consciousness, bypassing traditional barriers between worlds.

"They're adapting faster than we expected," Alice Chen said, appearing in his office doorway across several temporal variations. The mathematical equations behind her eyes tracked complex patterns of supernatural activity throughout Daybridge.

"The entities taught them how," Ethan replied, spreading out reports that existed in quantum superposition. "Not directly, but just by existing here, they showed the supernatural community new possibilities."

A map of Daybridge displayed on his modified computer screen, showing hotspots of paranormal temporal activity. The old cemetery where ghosts had learned to manifest across multiple timeline variations simultaneously. The forest preserve where fae creatures slipped between moments, turning temporal bleeding into doorways between realms. Abandoned buildings where darker things gathered, experimenting with reality's new malleability.

The latest report came from Dr. Patricia Rivera at the Department of Temporal Psychology: "Supernatural beings are demonstrating unprecedented adaptation to quantum consciousness states. Their natural affinity for non-conventional existence appears to be accelerating their ability to manipulate temporal mechanics."

Alice moved to the window, watching reality shift across the city skyline. "The chef at The Quantum Fork warned us this might happen. When consciousness learns to exist in multiple states..."

"Everything that lives between thoughts gets stronger," Ethan finished, remembering their conversations with the enigmatic chef.

His phone buzzed with a message from Ryan Matthew's team: "Reality bleeding detected at multiple supernatural gatherings. Pattern suggests coordinated activity."

A new set of photos appeared on his desk, showing impossible scenes. He spread them across his desk, each one more disturbing than the last. A vampire council meeting occurring across several timeline variations simultaneously. Werewolves hunting through temporal gaps, using quantum bleeding to track prey across multiple moments. Ancient spirits teaching younger supernatural beings how to exist between thoughts.

But it was the last photo that made both detectives pause – a gathering of various supernatural leaders, their forms shifting between states as they conducted what appeared to be a ritual involving temporal manipulation.

"They're organizing," Alice observed, the equations in her mind calculating possibilities. "Learning to use these new conditions to their advantage."

Ethan picked up a final report, its contents shifting between variations as he read. The classified supernatural temporal activity report detailed multiple species demonstrating advanced quantum consciousness manipulation, with evidence of coordinated efforts to exploit reality bleeding and possible connections to Class-3 entities. The warning at the bottom was clear: high probability of escalation.

"We need to talk to Nadia," Ethan said, watching shadows move unnaturally across his office walls. "If there's historical precedent for this..."

"Already scheduled," Alice confirmed. "The Archivist found references to similar patterns in ancient texts. Times when the supernatural world learned new ways to interact with reality."

Through his window, Ethan watched Daybridge shift between states of existence, its quantum-enhanced architecture glimmering with temporal energies. The city had adapted to its new reality, learned to thrive in a world where consciousness could exist in multiple states simultaneously.

But now something darker was stirring in the spaces between thoughts, in the gaps between moments where reality had grown thin. The supernatural community wasn't just adapting to these changes – they were learning to use them, to reshape them, to turn temporal bleeding into a weapon.

"Another case?" Marcus Wong asked from the doorway, his quantum-calibrated camera already capturing images that existed in multiple states.

"Something bigger," Alice replied, her enhanced perception tracking patterns that wove through reality itself. "The supernatural world is evolving, learning to exist between thoughts just like the entities. And some of them have plans for these new abilities."

Ethan gathered the shifting files, watching as reports wrote themselves across multiple timeline variations. In his enhanced perception, he could see darkness gathering between moments, feel ancient powers stirring in the gaps between thoughts.

The game was changing. The rules of reality had been rewritten, and now every creature that lived in the shadows was learning to play by these new rules. As night fell across multiple versions of Daybridge simultaneously, Ethan Reeves and Alice Chen prepared to face a world where supernatural beings had learned to exist in quantum superposition, where ancient powers moved through gaps in consciousness, and where the spaces between thoughts held darker secrets than anyone had imagined.

The next chapter was already writing itself across infinite possibilities, and somewhere in the quantum-shifted shadows of Daybridge, ancient eyes watched reality bleed between moments and waited.

A SNEAK PEEK AT WHAT'S NEXT!

Thank you for joining me on this journey through *Shadows Between Thoughts.* I hope you enjoyed exploring the mysteries of Daybridge and getting to know its secrets.

The story doesn't end here—there's so much more waiting to be uncovered. I'm excited to give you an exclusive first look at Quantum Detective: The Alice Chen Files, the next book in the *Ethan Reeves Werewolf Detective Series*. Dive into the free chapters below and get a taste of what's to come!

Quantum Detective: The Alice Chen Files Book Six in the Ethan Reeves Werewolf Detective Series

PROLOGUE: A PRESENT SHADOW

The dead body could wait. That thought alone should have alarmed Detective Alice Chen, but the wrongness pulsing through the abandoned warehouse demanded her full attention. Her breath crystallized in the November air, forming patterns that seemed to linger too long, defying the natural order of things. The warehouse loomed before her, a decrepit monument on the edge of the industrial district, its shadows moving in ways shadows shouldn't.

Something was wrong with the air – it felt thin, stretched like cellophane over forgotten furniture, vibrating with an energy that made her teeth ache. She'd felt temporal disturbances before, but this... this was like standing at the edge of a temporal tsunami.

"Detective Chen?" Officer Simons' voice cracked with nervous energy. "The coroner's en route. Should we proceed with—"

Alice raised her hand sharply, cutting him off. The younger officer's radio crackled with static, its frequency distorting as reality rippled around them. The warehouse façade flickered like a corrupted digital image – grimy windows suddenly pristine, rusted metal gleaming new, decades of decay reversing in heartbeats before snapping back.

"Stand back," she ordered, drawing her service weapon more from instinct than necessity. The familiar weight of the 9mm offered little comfort against the forces warping the fabric of time itself. "Nobody crosses this threshold."

The temporal distortion hit without warning, a psychic sledgehammer that dropped her to her knees. The warehouse dissolved like smoke in a wind that smelled of lightning and regret. Suddenly, she was walking the halls of the Police Academy – no, she was watching herself walk those halls, a younger Alice Chen with midnight hair pulled back in a severe bun and arms laden with case files. The dissociation was nauseating, like being simultaneously actor and audience in a play she'd performed years ago.

"You're late again, Cadet Chen!" The voice shattered through her like broken glass. Detective Denise Thompson materialized at the end of the corridor; her mentor's presence so vivid that Alice could smell her signature lavender perfume mixing with gun oil. Five years dead, but here she stood, arms crossed, dark eyes twinkling with that familiar mix of exasperation and pride.

"Sorry, Detective," young Alice stammered, and present-day Alice mouthed the words along with her past self, remembering the weight of those files, the burn of ambition. "I was reviewing the Robertson case files and—"

Reality convulsed. The academy's polished floors fractured, bleeding into the warehouse's crumbling concrete. Thompson's image stuttered like damaged film, her features dissolving into static before reforming into Officer Simons' concerned face. Past and present collided, temporal feedback howling in Alice's skull.

"Detective?" Simons' voice echoed strangely, as if traveling through water and decades simultaneously. "Jesus, you're bleeding..."

Alice touched her upper lip, fingers coming away red. She forced herself upright, using the doorframe for support as she holstered her weapon. The temporal echo was fading, leaving behind the taste of ozone and ancient copper pennies, along with something else – a metallic flavor she recognized from previous encounters with manipulated time. But this was stronger, more deliberate. This wasn't some random temporal anomaly; this was orchestrated.

"Call it in," she ordered, already pulling out her phone to text Ethan. Her fingers left bloody smears on the screen. "Tell dispatch we need PDU support immediately. Priority One temporal incident." She turned to Simons, seeing an echo of Thompson in his worried expression. "Nobody enters this building until they arrive. Something's actively manipulating time in there, and we're not equipped to handle it."

Her reflection in the warehouse windows fractured into multiple versions of herself – academy cadet, rookie cop, seasoned detective – before settling back into her current self. But for a moment, she could have sworn she saw a version she didn't recognize, older perhaps, or from a timeline that hadn't happened yet.

Time wasn't just broken here – it was being weaponized. Whatever entity was powerful enough to tear holes in reality had chosen this location, this moment, with deliberate purpose. The dead body inside suddenly seemed less like a crime scene and more like bait.

Alice pulled out her notebook, hands steady despite the psychic aftershocks still reverberating through her consciousness. She had work to do. The corpse might be able to wait, but whatever was fracturing time around it wouldn't. And she had a sickening feeling that this was just the beginning – that somewhere in the twisted temporal currents surrounding her, Denise Thompson's murder and this moment were connected by more than memory.

The warehouse door creaked on its hinges, pushed by a wind that smelled of the past and future colliding. Alice took a deep breath and stepped forward, into whatever nightmare waited within.

~

ABOUT THE AUTHOR

Rae Stonehouse turned to fiction writing after establishing himself as a prolific author of self-development and professional growth books.

With over 50 published works helping readers navigate personal and professional challenges, he embarked on a new creative path with the Ethan Reeves Werewolf Detective Series.

When not weaving tales of supernatural sleuthing, Stonehouse continues to share his expertise in personal development through workshops and speaking engagements from his home in British Columbia.

The Ethan Reeves series marks his debut in fiction writing, blending his understanding of human nature with a newfound passion for urban fantasy.

~